THE CONVERGENCE: BROKEN MAGIC

THE CONVERGENCE SERIES
BOOK 1

RICHARD FRENCH

ALSO BY RICHARD FRENCH

NON FICTION

The Art of Journaling

Write Your Way

Advanced Pattern Recognition

The Year End Reflection Guide

100 Self-Discovery Journaling Prompts

Revelation Explained: Verse by Verse

Proverbs for Profit

Daniel as a Blueprint for Navigating Ethical Dilemmas (2nd Edition)

FICTION

The Convergence: Broken Magic

The Convergence: Restoration

UNDER THE PEN NAME: RAVEN FONTAINE

The Shattered Crown

Sovereign Hearts

The Emotion Collector

Indie Pen Press

Turning Dreams into Best Sellers

Indie Pen Press
Seattle, Washington USA
IndiePenPress.com

Second Edition: June 2025

Paperback ISBN: 979-8-9991846-2-7

CONTENTS

PROLOGUE: THE PRICE OF POWER

Maria Smith's hands shook as golden light formed around her fingers. Through the Vigilant's window, darkness twisted against the stars—wrong darkness, hungry darkness, not the familiar empty space she knew.

"Energy readings are spiking." She gripped the control panel. The screens around her flickered as the ship's magic systems fought whatever lurked outside. "This isn't natural."

Captain James Foster tightened his grip on his chair. "Show me."

Maria pressed her palm to the controls. Golden light flowed from her hands into the ship—Luminor magic seeking connection. The ship's power responded like it remembered something. She'd read stories about old mages whose magic worked differently than today's rules allowed, but those were just stories.

Right?

A display materialized: shadow and light twisted together in patterns that broke apart and rebuilt themselves.

"Tenebral signatures detected," the ship's computer announced. "Warning: containment protocols failing."

The darkness pressed against the ship's hull, searching. Maria felt it through her link to the ship's systems—power older than anything they understood. Her golden energy shields began to crack.

"Full power to shields." Foster hit the emergency beacon. "Contact Federation Command—"

The window exploded.

Shadow poured through the breach, forming thick tentacles that reached for the crew.

Maria felt something impossible—her golden shields connecting with the dark energy. Like two pieces of something broken, trying to come back together. The sensation reminded her of stories about Haven Prime, where opposite magics had joined to fix broken reality.

She threw up a wall of golden light. The darkness slammed into it. She felt the blow through her whole body.

"Get down!" She poured more power into her shield while Foster hammered emergency buttons. Around them, other crew members ran to their stations, their magic blazing.

The shadows stopped. Pulled back. In their depths, Maria saw something that froze her blood—patterns in the chaos. Order in the madness. This wasn't random Tenebral energy.

It was thinking.

"Captain." Her voice shook. "This isn't some accident. Look at the patterns—it's organized, like—"

The darkness rushed forward again. Maria's shield shattered. Golden pieces of light scattered across the bridge as shadow flooded in. She saw Foster shouting orders and crew members casting protection spells.

Then the darkness touched her mind, and she saw what was coming.

Images filled her head: the first Convergence three hundred years ago in the Helios Sector, where reality had flickered between different states. Then the Meridian Incident fifty years later, when a whole colony reported their magic trying to merge. Each event stronger than the last, each pushing harder against the walls keeping magic separated. The Academy called them accidents, taught they were random breaks in the magic field.

But Maria saw the truth now. These weren't separate events— they were attempts. Like a cut trying to heal, reality had been reaching for something. Testing. Learning. And now, after hundreds of years of trying, it had broken through.

The Convergence was coming back. And this time, no one would be ready.

The patterns weren't about destroying—they were about changing. Like a doctor's blade, cutting to heal. The darkness wasn't eating reality. It was trying to remake it into something older. Something whole.

Maria's last act was to send a message toward Federation space, wrapped in golden light. As darkness took her, she hoped someone would understand the warning.

The Vigilant vanished into empty space, leaving only silence among the stars.

A thousand light-years away, on Zenith Prime, Samantha Reed woke with a start. Her room glowed with starlight. Golden magic danced around her fingers, responding to trouble she couldn't name.

Something was wrong with reality itself. And deep in her bones, she knew everything was about to change.

ONE
THE ENFORCER'S PATH

Samantha Reed knew three things with perfect certainty: Luminor magic flowed like water, the Federation preserved order, and her latest mission would test both truths.

She stood on the bridge of the Seraphine, watching golden light dance across her fingers. The ship's systems hummed in harmony with her magic, each crystal display pulsing in time with her heartbeat. This was control—what it meant to be a Federation enforcer.

The Academy's seven towers pierced the distance, their crystal spires catching morning light. Samantha's gaze lingered on the Unity Tower's darkened windows. During their final year, she and Connor had discovered old texts describing magic differently—not as separate forces but as parts of a single power. Their thesis project had explored ways to unite different magical approaches, earning them both praise and careful watching from the teachers.

"Some boundaries exist for a reason, Enforcer Reed," Williams had told her the day after Connor disappeared. She'd believed him then. Had to believe him. But watching those shadows writhe between lines of light on her tactical display, she felt the old questions stirring.

"Status report." She didn't turn from the window. Stars stretched before her—infinite possibilities in infinite darkness.

Emma Carter's voice carried from the tactical station, crisp and professional. "All systems normal, Commander. But there's something odd about these energy readings from Illyria."

Samantha crossed to Emma's station, studying the crystal display. Numbers and patterns scrolled past—a language as familiar to her as breathing. But Emma was right. Something was off. The magical signatures twisted in ways they shouldn't, defying the mathematical precision that defined Luminor energy.

"Show me the pattern analysis."

Emma's fingers danced across the controls, golden light flowing from her hands into the ship's systems. A three-dimensional model appeared: a web of energy lines spanning Illyria's surface. Most glowed with the steady light of controlled magic, but in one sector, shadows writhed between the lines.

Tenebral magic. The thought tightened Samantha's jaw. Shadow magic—the dark counterpart to her golden Luminor power. Not evil, the Academy taught, just different. Like two sides of the same coin that were never meant to touch.

"Looks like our intel was right." Emma's voice dropped almost to a whisper. "Connor Blake's been busy."

The name sent a chill down Samantha's spine. She'd studied the reports, memorized every detail about the rebel leader who'd turned his back on Federation training to embrace chaos. But seeing the evidence of his work—the way his Tenebral magic corrupted the natural flow of power—made it real in ways reports couldn't capture.

A memory surfaced: Late nights in the Academy's research lab, Connor's excitement infectious as they pushed the boundaries of acceptable magical theory. "Look at these resonance patterns," he'd said, golden light from her shields somehow harmonizing with his shadow constructs. "The frequencies shouldn't align like this, Sam. But they do. Why?"

They'd written it off as a quirk of their complementary magical styles. But now, years later, that memory carried weight she couldn't understand. Their experiments had worked too well, achieved results that defied standard magical theory. Results that had drawn Williams' personal attention.

"The council's waiting for your assessment." Emma glanced up from her station. "They're... eager for answers."

Of course they were. The council didn't like waiting, especially when Tenebral magic threatened their carefully maintained order. Samantha straightened.

"Open a channel to Council Chamber Alpha. Secure protocols."

The air shimmered as the holographic connection established itself. Twelve figures appeared, seated in a semicircle of floating chairs. Their faces were shadowed, but Samantha felt the weight of their attention.

"Enforcer Reed." Councilor Marcus Williams' voice filled the bridge. "Your report?"

Samantha gestured, sending the energy analysis floating into the shared space between them. "The situation on Illyria is worse than initial reports suggested. Blake isn't just experimenting with Tenebral magic—he's weaponizing it. These patterns show sophisticated manipulation of quantum fields, well beyond standard rebel capabilities."

"Concerning." Another councilor murmured. "The Federation cannot allow such power to remain unchecked."

"There's more." Samantha continued. "The energy signatures show similarities to the anomaly that destroyed the Vigilant."

A ripple of unease passed through the council. The loss of the Vigilant was still raw—a reminder that even the Federation's power had limits.

"Your recommendations?" Williams asked.

"A direct intervention. My team can—"

"No." The word cut through the chamber like a blade. Councilor Diana Reynolds leaned forward, her face catching the light. "This situation requires a more... permanent solution. You are authorized to use whatever force necessary to eliminate this threat."

Samantha felt Emma's surprise without looking at her. Eliminate, not capture. That wasn't standard protocol.

"Councilor—" Samantha chose her words carefully. "Blake's knowledge of Tenebral magic could be valuable. If we could bring him in—"

"Your loyalty to Federation protocol is admirable," Reynolds interrupted, "but these are not normal circumstances. The Convergence approaches, Enforcer Reed. We cannot afford half measures."

The Convergence. The word hung in the air like smoke. Samantha had heard whispers, seen fragments of classified reports. But for a councilor to speak of it openly...

"You have your orders," Williams said. "End this threat. Permanently."

The connection severed, leaving Samantha alone with her thoughts and the weight of command. She turned to find Emma watching her, concern evident in her expression.

"Things are worse than they're telling us." It wasn't a question.

Samantha's fingers traced the edge of the tactical display, golden light responding to her touch. "The council doesn't give kill orders lightly. Whatever Blake's planning, whatever connection it has to the Convergence..." She let the thought trail off.

"What's our move?"

Samantha studied the twisted energy patterns again, remembering her training. Luminor magic was about order, about maintaining the delicate balance that kept their civilization functioning. But as she watched shadows dance between lines of light, she couldn't shake the feeling that balance itself was changing.

"Set course for Illyria," she ordered. "And Emma, run a deep scan of those energy patterns. If the council isn't telling us everything, we need to know what we're really walking into."

As the Seraphine's engines hummed to life, Samantha felt the familiar surge of power flowing through the ship's crystal networks. But for the first time in her career, she wondered if maintaining order might require breaking it first.

The stars stretched into lines of light as they jumped to hyperspace, carrying them toward a confrontation that would change everything. Samantha only hoped she was ready for what awaited them on Illyria's surface.

She had to be. The alternative didn't bear thinking about.

The ship's tactical room was empty except for Samantha and Emma. They'd dismissed the rest of the command staff, needing privacy for what came next. Holographic displays surrounded them, each showing a different aspect of Illyria's magical topology. In the center, a three-dimensional map rotated slowly, shadow points marking Connor Blake's suspected movements.

"He's not random." Samantha studied the pattern. "Look here

and here." She traced lines between points of Tenebral activity. "He's creating a grid."

Emma leaned closer, her expression thoughtful. "A containment pattern? That's advanced theory. Most Tenebral users can barely maintain stable fields."

"Blake was top of his class at the Academy before he turned." Samantha pulled up his file, scanning details she'd already memorized. Perfect scores in theoretical applications. Innovation awards. Commendations from three different department heads. "He understood Luminor principles better than most. Makes him twice as dangerous now that he's corrupted them."

"You knew him." Emma's gaze fixed on her face.

Samantha's fingers stilled on the controls. "We trained together. Different years but the same advanced programs. He was..." She paused, choosing words carefully. "Brilliant. Intense. Always pushing boundaries, testing limits. The kind of student instructors dream of and dread in equal measure."

"What changed?"

"He found something in the restricted archives. I never learned what exactly—it's sealed beyond my clearance. But the next day, he was gone. Took half a dozen top students with him." Samantha's jaw tightened. "Three months later, they hit their first Federation facility. Seventeen dead. Forty-three injured. All because he decided order was a cage rather than a foundation."

Emma studied her face. "The council's kill order bothers you."

"It should bother everyone. We're enforcers, not executioners. There are protocols, procedures—"

"Which he's violated repeatedly. You've seen the casualty reports."

"That's not the point." Samantha gestured, expanding the tactical display. "Look at this pattern. He's planning something specific. Something big. We could be walking right into his endgame if we eliminate him without understanding what or why."

"You think the council's wrong?"

Dangerous question. Dangerous answer. Samantha chose her next words carefully. "I think they're not telling us everything. The Convergence, the Vigilant's destruction, Blake's pattern here—it's all connected, but they're giving us pieces instead of the whole picture."

"So what do we do about it?"

Samantha smiled, but there was no warmth in it. "We follow orders. Mostly. Computer, run simulation alpha seven. Full tactical overlay."

The holographic display shifted, becoming a real-time battle simulation. Ghostly figures moved through constructed scenarios, magic flaring in predictable patterns.

"Standard Federation response protocols." Samantha narrated as the scene played out. "Containment perimeter. Magical suppression fields. Direct confrontation." The simulation ended with Blake's capture. "That's what they'll expect us to do. And that's exactly why it won't work."

Emma raised an eyebrow. "You have something else in mind?"

Samantha studied the tactical display. "Blake thinks like a tactician. He'll have counters prepared for every standard approach. But there's one thing he won't expect." Her fingers danced over the controls, modifying the simulation. "We're going to let him think he's winning."

The new scenario played out, showing a very different engagement. Emma watched with growing understanding. "A trap within a trap. If he thinks we're following standard protocols—"

"He'll be looking for the obvious double-cross, not the triple-cross underneath." Samantha zoomed in on a particular sequence. "We'll need perfect timing. If any element is off by even a second—"

The tactical room door slid open. Lieutenant Ryan Marshall stood in the doorway, his expression tense. "Commander. We're picking up a transmission from Illyria. You need to see this."

Samantha exchanged glances with Emma. "Put it through."

The tactical displays cleared, replaced by a static-filled transmission. When it cleared, Samantha's breath caught. Connor Blake's face filled the screen, older than his Academy photos but still recognizable. Still dangerous.

"This message is for the Federation Council." He began, his voice carrying the same intensity Samantha remembered. "You sent your enforcers to stop me. To maintain your precious order. But you don't understand what's coming. The Convergence isn't just another magical anomaly—it's a reckoning, a force that will break the chains you've placed on reality itself."

He leaned closer to the camera, and Samantha saw shadows writhing in his eyes. "Your time is ending. The old laws, the old limits—all of it will burn in the fire of true freedom. And there's nothing your pet enforcers can do to stop it."

The transmission cut off. For a moment, no one spoke.

"Well," Emma said finally, "that complicates things."

Samantha stared at the space where Blake's face had been, her mind racing through tactical adjustments. "No. This is good. He's trying to provoke a response, which means—"

"He's ready to move." Emma finished. "The grid pattern, the public challenge..."

"It's starting." Samantha straightened, decision made. "Lieutenant Marshall, begin mission prep: full combat load-out, plus magical containment gear. Emma, I want triple redundancy on our containment fields. If Blake wants to talk about breaking chains, we'll give him something to break against."

As her officers moved to comply, Samantha turned back to the tactical display. Somewhere on Illyria, Connor Blake was preparing to reshape reality. She had orders to stop him permanently. But first, she needed answers.

The council was hiding something. Blake knew what it was. And one way or another, she would find out the truth—even if she had to break a few protocols to do it.

The game was changing. Time to change with it.

TWO

THE SHADOW'S DANCE

Connor Blake stood in the heart of the rebel base, watching shadows dance across his skin. Tenebral magic responded to his every thought, twisting reality in ways the Federation claimed were impossible.

He'd seen it first in the Academy archives—records of paired mages whose powers resonated in impossible ways. Teams that achieved results far beyond their individual abilities. The Federation had labeled them aberrations and buried the reports in restricted files. But Connor had recognized the pattern: souls finding each other across artificial boundaries, magic remembering its original state.

The Federation's control extended through seventeen sectors, each governed by a regional council that answered to the high council on Zenith Prime. Their power was built on more than political structure—it was anchored in the very division of magic itself, a separation maintained through carefully structured laws, education, and rigid enforcement.

But that control was slipping. Reports crossed his desk daily: Luminor and Tenebral practitioners forming working pairs without instruction, achieving effects that shouldn't have been possible. A training facility in the outer sectors where students' magic had started merging on its own. Even here in his own base, he watched as certain teams naturally gravitated together, their powers harmonizing in ways that reminded him of old patterns—of experiments performed late at night with golden light dancing against shadow.

The training chamber's crystal walls absorbed his excess energy, preventing detection by Federation sensors. Not that it mattered now. His message to the council had made secrecy pointless. Let them come. Let them see what true freedom looked like.

"The Federation fleet's changing course." Rachel Thompson's voice carried from her monitoring station. Shadows clung to her uniform, a sign of prolonged Tenebral exposure. "They're pushing their engines hard. Estimate arrival in fifteen minutes."

Connor nodded, unsurprised. "Samantha Reed doesn't waste time." He'd known they'd send her. The Federation's perfect enforcer, their symbol of controlled power. If they only knew what was coming.

"You sure about this?" Rachel stepped away from her station, keeping her voice low. "Once we start, there's no going back. The Convergence—"

"Will reshape everything." Connor pulled more shadows around himself, feeling reality bend. "The Federation built their precious order on a foundation of lies. Time they learned the truth."

Rachel studied the tactical display, where red dots marked Federation ship positions. "And what about the civilians? When we trigger the grid, the effects will—"

"Be contained." Connor's voice left no room for debate. "I've calculated every variable, planned for every contingency. The grid will hold."

He turned to the massive holomap dominating the chamber's center. Illyria's capital sprawled before him in miniature, key points marked with pulsing shadows. The grid pattern was beautiful in its complexity—months of work hidden in plain sight. The Federation thought they were tracking random Tenebral activity. They didn't see the larger pattern, the mathematical precision underlying apparent chaos.

Just like the Academy had never seen it, even when he'd tried to show them.

The truth had been there all along, hidden in plain sight. Every successful magical partnership throughout history showed the same underlying resonance patterns. He saw it now in the grid's design—how each node sought its counterpart, light and shadow, reaching for each other like muscle memory of an older form. The Federation's forced separation was like a dam holding back a river. But water always remembers its natural course.

In quiet moments, he felt Samantha's presence in the mathematics of it all. Their research had come closer than anyone to understanding the truth—that unified souls weren't an aberration but reality trying to heal itself. He wondered if she felt it too, that pull toward something older than Federation doctrine.

"Team leads report ready," Rachel said, interrupting his thoughts. "But Jackson's group is showing signs of strain. The Tenebral exposure—"

"Is necessary." Connor crossed to her station, studying the medical readouts. "Their bodies are adapting. The ones who can't handle it will be evacuated before we begin."

Rachel's expression tightened. "Like the others?"

He met her gaze steadily. "The cost was explained. Everyone here chose to be part of something greater than themselves."

"And what about her?" Rachel nodded toward the tactical display, where the Seraphine's marker approached. "Will she understand the cost?"

Connor's fingers traced the ship's trajectory. Samantha Reed, the Federation's sword of justice, was coming to restore order. She'd been brilliant at the Academy—passionate, driven, absolutely certain of her path. Just like him before he'd found the truth.

"She'll understand," he said quietly. "Once she sees what I've seen, what the Federation's been hiding all these years."

The base's alert system pulsed: a warning from its outer sensors. Connor returned to the holomap, watching new data flow in. The Seraphine was pushing its engines beyond safety limits. Samantha must have seen the energy readings from the city, must have realized something bigger was happening.

Good. He needed her sharp. Needed her to see past Federation doctrine to the fundamental truth he'd discovered in those restricted archives.

"Begin evacuation of non-essential personnel," he ordered. "Move the sensitives to the shielded bunkers. And bring me the containment readings from sectors seven through twelve."

As Rachel relayed his orders, Connor reached out with his Tenebral senses. The grid hummed with potential energy, each node perfectly placed. When activated, it would create a resonance pattern unlike anything the Federation had seen before—a pattern that would expose the truth about magic itself.

The shadows around him writhed faster, responding to his anticipation. Most users found Tenebral magic difficult to control, its chaotic nature fighting any attempt at direction. But Connor had learned its secret: you didn't control chaos. You became part of it, let it flow through you, guide you toward possibilities that order denied.

"Sir?" One of the younger rebels—Michael Sims—approached with a data tablet. "We're getting strange readings from the Convergence monitors. The patterns are... shifting."

Connor took the tablet and studied the displays. Energy patterns twisted across the screen, beautiful in their complexity. But Michael was right—something had changed. The Convergence was moving faster than his calculations had predicted.

They were running out of time.

"Move up the timetable," he ordered. "Begin grid activation sequence. Alert all teams—we start in ten minutes."

Rachel's head snapped up. "Ten minutes? But the civilian evacuation—"

"Won't be complete. I know." Connor's fingers clenched around the tablet. "But if we wait, we lose our window. The Convergence is accelerating. If we don't channel it properly..."

He let the thought hang. They all knew the stakes. The Federation wanted to control the Convergence and use it to cement their power forever. They didn't understand that trying to control that kind of power would tear reality apart.

Better a controlled burn than a wildfire.

"What about Reed?" Rachel asked. "She'll be in range when we activate."

"That's part of the plan." Connor moved to the chamber's main control panel, shadows swirling around his hands as he began the activation sequence. "She needs to see this, to understand what's really happening."

Samantha Reed wasn't just another enforcer; she was the key to everything—the one person whose power and position could make the Federation listen. If he could show her the truth, make her understand what he'd discovered...

The base rumbled as massive generators spun up, feeding power to the grid. On the holomap, shadow points pulsed in sequence, the pattern spreading across the city like a web of darkness. Years of planning and careful preparation all came down to this moment.

"All teams report ready," Rachel announced. "Grid power at eighty percent and rising."

Connor closed his eyes, feeling the surge of Tenebral energy through the grid. The shadows around him sang with potential, with the promise of change. The Federation thought they were fighting to preserve order. They didn't understand that sometimes order had to break for something better to emerge.

"Seraphine entering weapons range," Rachel reported. "They're charging weapons. Sir... what do we do if she doesn't understand, if she can't see past her training?"

Connor opened his eyes, watching the Seraphine's approach on the tactical display. "She'll understand. Unlike the rest of the Federation, Samantha Reed always puts truth before doctrine. Even at the Academy, she questioned everything, pushed every boundary."

"And if you're wrong?"

The question hung in the air as Connor initiated the final activation sequence. On the holomap, the grid pattern blazed with shadow fire as reality itself began to bend.

"Then we all lose," he said quietly. "Because without her, what comes next will destroy everything."

The grid hummed with power, ready to reshape reality itself. In ten minutes, nothing would ever be the same.

Connor Blake smiled into the gathering darkness. It was time to show the Federation what real power looked like.

The dance was about to begin.

THREE
CONFLICTING CURRENTS

The Seraphine's landing thrusters kicked up storms of dust as it touched down on Illyria's surface. Through the viewscreen, Samantha watched golden shields deflect debris from the hull, her magic maintaining precise control despite the turbulence. Everything by protocol, even as the world fell apart around them.

"Grid activation detected," Emma reported from tactical. "The pattern... it's spreading across the city."

Samantha studied the readings, mouth tight. Connor's work was beautiful, in a terrifying way. Each shadow point was placed with mathematical precision, creating a web of Tenebral energy that defied conventional theory. This wasn't chaos—it was orchestrated disruption.

"Teams ready?" she asked, though she already knew the answer. Emma wouldn't have it any other way.

"Armed and waiting. Jackson's squad reports unusual energy readings from the target zone. They're saying—"

The ship's sensors screamed. The fabric of existence buckled around them as the first wave of Connor's grid activated. Samantha threw up a barrier of golden light instinctively, feeling the pressure of twisted space press against her magic.

"Move now," she ordered. "All teams deploy. Standard formation, modified containment protocols. And Emma, watch the shadows. Blake's not playing by any rulebook today."

They emerged into chaos. The city's architecture writhed, buildings stretching and contracting as Tenebral energy rewrote local physics. Civilians ran screaming from advancing walls of shadow while emergency responders tried futilely to maintain order.

Samantha's team moved with practiced precision, golden shields creating safe corridors through the chaos. She felt Connor's presence ahead—a dark star in her magical senses, pulling at the fabric of reality itself.

"Commander!" Jackson's voice crackled over the comm. "We've got rebels on the east approach. They're—" Static burst through the channel.

"Jackson? Report!" Samantha stretched her senses toward his last position. Nothing but twisted space and shadow.

"Ma'am." Emma pointed toward a nearby building. Its windows had become mirrors, reflecting impossible angles. "Look."

In the distorted glass, Samantha saw them—Jackson's team, frozen in mid-motion as reality warped around them. Not dead, but caught in a moment of stretched time. Connor's work again. He'd learned new tricks since the Academy.

"Can we break them out?" Emma asked.

Samantha studied the distortion. "Not without understanding

the math behind it. Blake's using unified field principles—if we disrupt it wrong, we could collapse the local space-time metric."

"Since when does Tenebral magic follow mathematical rules?"

"Since Connor Blake decided to rewrite them." Samantha pressed her hand against the glass, feeling the equations beneath. "He's not destroying order—he's creating a new one. Which means..."

She spun, sword materializing in her hand as shadows coalesced behind them. Rachel Thompson emerged from the darkness, other rebels flanking her.

"Commander Reed," Rachel said, shadows writhing around her uniform. "Connor's waiting for you."

Samantha's blade hummed with stored power. "Release my people."

"They're safer where they are. The Convergence is coming. What happens next..." Rachel's eyes flickered to the twisted sky. "You need to understand before it's too late."

"Understand what? That Blake's torn reality apart? That he's—"

"That the Federation lied to us all." Connor's voice cut through the chaos. He stepped out of a shadow portal, magic rolling off him in waves. "About everything."

Samantha shifted her stance, blade ready. "Last time we met, you killed seventeen people. Gave me a scar to remember you by."

"And you gave me one to match." Connor's hand touched his side, where her blade had struck. "But this isn't about our past. Look around you, Sam. Really look. What do you see?"

Despite herself, Samantha looked past the chaos, past the terror to the underlying pattern. Connor's grid wasn't random. It was...

"Impossible," she breathed. The mathematics clicked into place.

"You're creating a resonance cascade. Using the Convergence itself to—"

"To show the truth." Connor stepped closer. "Luminor, Tenebral—they're not opposites. They're the same force, split by the Federation's lies. The Convergence isn't an accident. It's reality trying to heal itself."

"By tearing itself apart?"

"Sometimes healing hurts." Connor raised his hand, shadows swirling. "The Federation found something, Sam—in those sealed archives. Something that changed everything. Why do you think they sent you to kill me? Why give that order now when the Convergence approaches?"

Samantha's blade dipped slightly. "How do you know about those orders?"

"Because I know how they think, how they operate." Connor's eyes met hers, and she saw the same intensity that had drawn her to him at the Academy. "They're scared, Sam. Not of me, not of the rebels. They're scared of what happens when everyone learns the truth."

"What truth?"

The grid pulsed. Reality screamed. And at that moment, as golden light met shadow, Samantha felt it—the resonance between their magic, the impossible harmony of order and chaos combined.

"That's not possible," she whispered.

"Isn't it?" Connor held out his hand, palm up. Shadows danced above it, forming complex patterns. "Your Luminor magic feels it too, doesn't it? The connection. The potential. We're not enemies, Sam. We're proof that both types of magic can work together, can heal what the Federation broke."

"Commander!" Emma's voice was urgent. "The grid's reaching critical levels. If we don't stop it—"

"We all die," Connor finished. "Unless we work together. The Convergence is coming, Sam. Reality itself is trying to reunite what was split apart. We can help it happen safely or watch it tear everything apart." He met her eyes. "Your choice."

Samantha felt the power building around them and saw the equations playing out in the twisted air. Connor's grid wasn't just reshaping local space—it was creating a template, a pattern for reality itself to follow.

If he was right...

If the Federation had lied...

"Commander!" Emma raised her weapon as more rebels emerged from the shadows. "Orders?"

Samantha stared at Connor's outstretched hand, feeling the weight of everything balanced at this moment. Protocol said to strike him down, and training said to contain the threat.

But the magic itself...

The magic told a different story.

"Hold position," she ordered. "Something's not right here. We need to—"

Reality twisted. The grid pulsed with new power. And in that moment, as golden light met shadow, Samantha Reed saw what Connor Blake had discovered in those sealed archives.

The truth about everything.

"Oh God," she whispered. "What have they done?"

The dance of light and shadow continued, and the world held its breath for what came next.

FOUR
THE WEIGHT OF ORDERS

Samantha's hands trembled as she spread Connor Blake's Academy file across her desk. The familiar quarters aboard the Seraphine had never felt so confining, the walls pressing closer with each piece of evidence that refused to make sense.

The official records painted Connor as a brilliant student who had turned violent without warning. But brilliant students didn't just snap. Samantha had seen enough tactical profiles to know the difference between calculated transformation and genuine psychological breakdown.

She pulled up security footage from his final week at the Academy. In every frame, Connor looked exhausted. Hunted. Dark circles under his eyes, shoulders rigid with tension, glancing over his shoulder as if expecting pursuit.

This wasn't how someone planning rebellion would act. This was someone who had discovered something that terrified him.

"Computer, show Connor Blake's library records and research files for his final semester."

"Access denied. Insufficient clearance."

Samantha's fingers froze on the controls. The words hit her like a physical blow. She was a Federation Enforcer with Level 7 access —clearance that let her review classified materials, tactical databases, enforcement protocols. And she couldn't see a student's library records?

Her tactical training kicked in, pattern recognition skills drilled into her until they became instinct. When something didn't make sense, there was usually a reason. Usually a dangerous one.

"Display my current access level."

"Level 7 clearance confirmed. Access to classified materials, tactical databases, and enforcement protocols authorized."

"Display Connor Blake's final academy project security level."

"Level 9 restriction. Council authorization required."

Level 9. Samantha leaned back in her chair, mind racing through the security classifications she'd memorized during training. Level 9 clearance was reserved for existential threats to Federation security—weapons capable of destroying entire sectors, experiments that could break reality itself.

What had a student been researching that warranted that level of secrecy?

The question sent a chill down her spine. She pulled up Connor's academic progression records, looking for clues. Top scores in theoretical applications. Innovation awards from three different departments. Glowing recommendations from instructors who had taught for decades.

This was the trajectory of a student destined for the Council itself, not exile and rebellion.

Then, in his final semester, everything changed.

The shift was dramatic. Project classifications jumped to restricted levels. Instructor notes became terse and formal. The enthusiastic recommendations vanished, replaced by careful bureaucratic language that said nothing while implying everything dangerous.

"Computer, display instructor evaluations for Connor Blake, final semester."

The records scrolled past, each one more troubling than the last. Professor Martinez: "Student shows concerning interest in theoretical applications beyond approved curricula." Dr. Lloyd: "Recommend monitoring for potential security issues." Williams himself: "Exceptional aptitude requires careful guidance to prevent misapplication."

Misapplication. Samantha highlighted the word, pulse quickening. She cross-referenced it with Academy terminology databases. The official definition seemed harmless enough—using magical theory inappropriately or unsafely.

But Williams had used the same term in seventeen other student files over the past decade.

She pulled up those records, throat tightening as the pattern emerged.

Every single student had either transferred to remote assignments or vanished from Academy records entirely.

The realization hit her like a physical blow. This wasn't random academic failure or normal career progression. This was planned removal of students who had discovered something they weren't supposed to know.

But what could be so dangerous that the Federation would eliminate their own brightest minds?

"Computer, display Connor Blake's research partner assignments, final semester."

"Samantha Reed, Advanced Theoretical Applications."

Her own name stared back at her from the screen. For a moment, the world seemed to tilt. She remembered that semester with painful clarity now—the excitement of pushing boundaries, the thrill of discovering new applications for unified field theory. She and Connor had worked together like two halves of a greater mind, their different approaches to magic complementing each other in ways that surprised even their instructors.

They had been investigating theoretical applications of unified magic—the possibility that Luminor and Tenebral energies weren't truly separate forces but different aspects of a single, more fundamental power. Their research had produced results that shouldn't have been possible according to Federation doctrine.

Results that had made their instructors nervous.

Results that Williams had personally shut down.

The memories came flooding back now, details she hadn't thought about in years. Late nights in the research lab, Connor's infectious enthusiasm as they achieved breakthrough after breakthrough. The moment when they realized their unified field equations were producing effects that violated basic assumptions about magical separation.

The equations had been beautiful—elegant mathematical proofs that suggested the artificial nature of the barriers between Luminor and Tenebral energies. As if someone had deliberately split what was meant to be whole.

"Computer, display sealed project files for Samantha Reed, final semester Academy training."

"Access denied. Level 9 clearance required."

Her own research. Classified at the same level as existential threats to Federation security.

The room felt airless. What had she and Connor discovered in those late-night research sessions that had been deemed too dangerous for even her to remember? She tried to recall specific details from their project, but the memories felt distant, viewed through a mental fog that hadn't been there before.

That observation triggered a new line of inquiry that made her stomach turn.

Samantha accessed her personal medical records from Academy graduation, scanning through the routine documentation with new eyes. Standard psychological evaluations, health screenings, the usual bureaucratic processing.

But there was an anomaly—a three-day gap in her schedule during the final week of classes. No courses, no examinations, no official activities recorded. Just a clinical notation: "Special administrative processing."

"Computer, cross-reference 'special administrative processing' with Academy medical protocols."

"Restricted information. Level 8 clearance required."

Level 8. Higher than her current authorization, but not as high as Connor's research classification. The pattern was becoming terrifyingly clear.

Memory modification protocols existed—she knew that much from her tactical training. They were used on deep cover operatives, on individuals who had been exposed to classified information they couldn't be allowed to retain. The Federation taught that consciousness was sacred, that mental autonomy was one of the fundamental rights they existed to protect.

But if they were willing to modify the memories of their own students...

The thought made her physically ill. Had they stolen her memories? Had they removed her recollection of whatever she and Connor had discovered together? Was her entire understanding of her own past built on carefully constructed lies?

"Commander?" Emma's voice came through the comm, startling her from her spiraling thoughts. "We're receiving updated intelligence on Blake's activities. Could you review the tactical assessment?"

"Send it to my terminal," Samantha replied, grateful for anything that might anchor her to the present. "I'll review it shortly."

But instead of studying the tactical data, she found herself staring at Connor's Academy photo. Young, enthusiastic, brilliant—everything the Federation claimed to value in its future leaders. His eyes held the same passionate curiosity she remembered from their research sessions.

What had transformed him from that eager student into the figure now described as a terrorist threatening Federation stability?

She pulled up his instructor evaluations again, this time studying the language patterns with new understanding. The early reviews showed genuine admiration: "exceptional analytical capabilities," "innovative theoretical insights," "natural leadership potential."

The later ones told a different story: "requires guidance," "potential security concerns," "recommend monitoring."

The shift hadn't been gradual. It had happened over the course of three weeks, coinciding exactly with the period when their joint research project had been producing its most significant results.

Samantha closed her eyes, forcing herself to push through the mental fog that surrounded those final weeks at the Academy. Fragments emerged like pieces of a shattered mirror—Connor's excitement as they achieved results that defied explanation, the moment they realized their equations suggested something fundamentally wrong with accepted magical theory.

She remembered Williams' visit to their lab with new clarity. He had seemed pleased initially, asking detailed questions about their methodology, their results, their theoretical frameworks. But his expression had changed when Connor showed him their latest findings—mathematical proofs that suggested Luminor and Tenebral energies weren't naturally separate but had been artificially divided.

"Fascinating work," Williams had said, his voice carefully neutral despite the tension in his shoulders. "You'll need to document everything thoroughly for review. I'll arrange for a special evaluation committee to assess your findings."

Three days later, Connor was gone. Their research was classified beyond her clearance level. And Samantha had undergone "special administrative processing" that she couldn't clearly remember.

The tactical report Emma had sent contained updated energy readings from Illyria. Samantha forced herself to focus on the data, but what she saw there only confirmed her growing suspicions. The energy signatures Blake was generating showed mathematical elegance that spoke of deep theoretical understanding. These weren't the chaotic emissions of a rogue terrorist —they were the controlled applications of someone who understood unified field theory at a fundamental level.

Someone who had been systematically trained in theoretical applications before being forced into exile.

Someone whose brilliance had made him too dangerous to the Federation's carefully maintained order.

The secure communication terminal chimed with an incoming priority message. Council authorization codes flashed across the screen, followed by Councilor Reynolds' stern image.

"Commander Reed," Reynolds said, her voice carrying the full weight of institutional authority. "I trust you're making good progress toward your objective."

"We're approaching the target zone now," Samantha replied carefully, keeping her voice steady despite the turmoil in her thoughts. "Blake's activities show more sophistication than initial reports suggested."

Something flickered across Reynolds' expression—not surprise, but calculation. "All the more reason to complete your mission quickly. The longer Blake remains active, the more damage he can do to Federation stability."

Reynolds leaned forward slightly, and Samantha caught the subtle emphasis in her next words. "I want to stress the importance of following your orders exactly, Commander. This situation requires decisive action, not prolonged analysis."

The warning was diplomatically phrased but unmistakably clear: Don't think too hard about what you're being asked to do.

"Understood, Councilor. Is there additional intelligence I should be aware of?"

"Only that Blake's research at the Academy touched on classified areas that remain sensitive to Federation security. His current activities suggest he's attempting to apply theoretical knowledge in ways that could destabilize the magical frameworks maintaining interstellar civilization."

Reynolds' expression hardened, and for a moment, Samantha saw something like fear in the older woman's eyes. "He cannot be allowed to continue."

The connection terminated, leaving Samantha alone with her thoughts and a growing certainty that she was being fed carefully selected portions of the truth.

She opened Connor's Academy file again, this time focusing on the psychological evaluations from his final semester. The pattern was subtle but consistent—gradual documentation of "concerning ideological drift," "questions about institutional authority," "potential reliability issues."

But when she compared those evaluations with his academic performance metrics, another picture emerged. Connor's work had remained consistently excellent throughout the period when his psychological fitness was being questioned. His research had continued to produce significant breakthroughs even as his instructors expressed growing concerns about his loyalty.

It was as if two different people were being documented—the brilliant researcher whose work advanced Federation knowledge, and the potential security threat whose questions made his superiors uncomfortable.

The same pattern appeared in her own psychological evaluations from that period. Her tests showed "excellent adaptation to institutional expectations" and "strong alignment with Federation values." But reading between the lines, she understood what that really meant: she had learned to stop asking the wrong questions.

Unlike Connor, she had been successfully processed by the system. Her curiosity had been channeled into acceptable directions, her loyalty secured through careful application of institutional pressure and, apparently, selective memory modification.

The thought that her own mind had been tampered with should have filled her with rage. Instead, she felt a cold analytical clarity settling over her—the same focused calm that came over her in combat situations when emotions became a liability.

If the Federation was willing to modify the memories of their own students, if they were systematically eliminating individuals who discovered inconvenient truths, then everything she had believed about their mission and methods was built on deception.

Connor Blake wasn't a terrorist who had betrayed his training. He was someone who had discovered the truth and been punished for it.

Her orders were to eliminate him—not to understand his motivations, not to assess the validity of his claims, just to remove a problem that threatened institutional stability.

But Samantha had spent seven years as an enforcer precisely because she believed in truth over convenience, justice over expedience. The Federation had trained her to think analytically, to question assumptions, to pursue evidence wherever it led.

They had failed to consider what would happen when she applied those skills to the Federation itself.

"Computer, compile all available data on Academy students who have been transferred or removed from active service over the past fifteen years. Focus on advanced theoretical programs."

"Compilation complete. Warning: extensive data classified at levels exceeding current authorization."

"Display what's available at my clearance level."

The results painted a picture that made her throat constrict. Dozens of brilliant students, all following similar patterns—exceptional performance followed by sudden "reliability concerns" and subsequent removal from Federation service. The mathematical consistency suggested systematic processing rather than individual decisions.

At the center of it all was Williams—the Academy's chief administrator, the man who had personally overseen the classification of her research with Connor.

The man who had given her current orders to eliminate the threat Blake represented.

Samantha stood and walked to the viewport, watching stars streak past as the Seraphine continued toward Illyria. In a few hours, she would confront Connor Blake, carrying orders to kill someone who might be the only person left who remembered what they had discovered together.

The weight of that realization settled on her shoulders like a physical burden. How many other brilliant minds had been silenced to protect the Federation's secrets? How many potential allies had she helped eliminate, believing she was serving justice when she was actually serving control?

Her comm chimed with another message from Emma. "Commander, we're detecting unusual energy patterns ahead. Whatever Blake is doing, it's bigger than our initial projections suggested."

"Acknowledged. I'll be on the bridge shortly."

Samantha took one last look at Connor's file, committing the young man's face to memory. Somewhere beneath the layers of institutional processing and selective memory modification, she had once known him as a partner in discovery, someone who shared her passion for pushing boundaries and uncovering truth.

Tomorrow, she would have to choose between the loyalty she

owed to the Federation and the loyalty she owed to that shared commitment to truth.

For the first time in her career as an enforcer, she wasn't certain which choice she would make.

But she was certain of one thing: whatever decision she reached would be based on complete information rather than comfortable lies.

The Academy had made a crucial error in their processing. They had taught her to value truth above all else, then expected her to accept deception when it served institutional interests.

Some lessons, once learned, could never be unlearned.

Even when forgetting might have been safer.

FIVE
BREAKING POINT

R eality screamed around them as Connor's grid pulsed with increasing power. The truth Samantha had seen—the impossible revelation in those patterns—threatened to shatter everything she'd ever believed.

Through their merged consciousness, she felt how their magic touched reality differently than Williams' forced experiments. Where his power left burning scars in space-time, theirs seemed to awaken something dormant. The very fabric of reality responded to their unified magic like parched earth receiving rain, absorbing and amplifying their power in ways that defied Federation physics.

She remembered the Academy's documented attempts at unification—sterile laboratories where they'd forced Luminor and Tenebral energies to combine. Those experiments had always ended the same way: reality fracturing under the strain, magic itself rejecting the artificial merger. But here, now, reality wasn't breaking under their touch—it was breathing.

But there wasn't time to process it, not with the fabric of space itself starting to tear.

41

"The resonance is building," Connor said, his voice tight with concentration. Shadows writhed around him, trying to contain the cascading energies. "If we don't stabilize it—"

"I know." Samantha's mind raced through calculations, through years of training proved wrong. "Emma, get our teams back. Minimum safe distance."

Emma didn't move. "Commander, protocol requires—"

"Protocol is what got us here." Samantha met her second's eyes. "Trust me."

There was a moment's hesitation, then Emma nodded sharply. She began barking orders into her comm, directing their forces to fall back. Rachel Thompson did the same with the rebel teams, though her shadows never stopped swirling defensively.

"The grid's approaching critical," Connor said. "We need to—"

The air split open.

A tear in reality appeared between them, its edges crackling with combined energies. Through it, Samantha caught glimpses of something else—other places, other times. Connor's grid's mathematical precision was breaking down under the strain of containing too much power.

"How do we stop it?" she demanded.

"We don't." Connor's shadows probed the tear's edges, trying to hold them steady. "But we can redirect it. If we combine our power—"

"The way they did before?" The knowledge she'd glimpsed burned in her mind. "That's what destroyed—"

She saw the patterns forming before he finished speaking. Unlike Williams' brutal channeling that left reality bleeding at the edges, their combined power created matrices of perfect symmetry. The mathematical beauty of it struck her—where artificial unification produced fractured, corrupted formulas, their natural unity wrote equations that made reality sing.

The evidence was right there in the tear itself. The areas they touched began to stabilize, not through force but through resonance, like a crystal finding its natural structure. While Williams' power left marks of trauma on space-time, their unified magic seemed to remind reality of its true nature.

"This is different. We know what we're doing. They didn't." He met her eyes. "Sam, there's no time. The resonance pattern is collapsing. Either we work together, or everyone in this city dies."

She knew he was right. They could feel it in the way reality shuddered around them. The Federation had lied about so much, but the fundamental physics were undeniable. Without intervention, the cascade would tear Illyria apart.

"Emma," she said quietly, "get everyone clear. If this doesn't work..."

"Commander—"

"That's an order."

Emma's expression hardened, but she nodded. As she retreated with the others, Samantha turned to Connor. "How do we do this?"

"Like at the Academy. Remember the unified field exercises, before they shut down the program?" He held out his hand, shadows dancing. "Your light, my shadow. They were never meant to be separate."

Samantha hesitated only a moment before reaching out. Golden light met writhing darkness, and the power that surged between them took her breath away. This wasn't the careful, controlled magic she'd been taught. This was something older. Something real.

In the distance, she could see the effects of Williams' corruption—Federation soldiers moving like broken puppets as artificially unified magic tore through them. Their power left traces of wrongness, like oil floating on water, never truly combining. But where their forced unity created discord, her connection with Connor resonated with mathematical perfection. Each pulse of their magic sent ripples through local space-time that didn't damage reality's structure but rather seemed to remind it of its original pattern.

Through their combined senses, they felt the difference in the underlying equations. Williams' methods tried to force new laws onto reality. Their unified magic revealed what had always been there, hidden beneath centuries of artificial separation.

Unlike Williams' forced combinations of power that left his soldiers twisted and broken, their magic merged like two halves of a melody finding harmony. Samantha felt the difference in her bones. Where artificial unification created discord, this felt like remembering—as if their magic had always known how to dance together, had just been waiting for them to stop fighting it.

Through their combined power, she glimpsed patterns that echoed formulas she'd once found in restricted texts: recursive loops of energy that transformed rather than destroyed, magical matrices that spoke of wholeness rather than division. The Federation taught that such combinations would tear reality apart. But this... this felt like reality finally making sense.

Together, they faced the tear in reality. Connor's shadows provided structure, while Samantha's light filled the gaps, creating a new kind of pattern—not order or chaos, but something in between, something whole.

She'd seen other attempts at combining Luminor and Tenebral magic—Williams' brutal forcing of power through unwilling vessels, the Academy's sterile experiments with mechanically merged energies. All had produced the same results: fractured magic, broken practitioners, shattered reality.

But this was different. Where forced unification created jagged edges and bleeding wounds in the fabric of space-time, their combined power moved like living water, seeking cracks and smoothing them whole. The mathematics underlying their magic didn't speak of domination or control—it sang of restoration, of pieces remembering they were meant to be one.

The tear fought them. Reality itself seemed to rebel against their effort to reshape it.

No, Samantha realized, not rebelling—responding. Like a wound finally receiving proper treatment after years of wrong medicine. Each pulse of their unified magic drew answering rhythms from the surrounding space, harmonics she recognized from their old Academy research. The patterns they'd discovered late at night in forbidden experiments weren't theoretical abstractions—they were reality's blueprint, showing how things were meant to be.

She felt Connor reach the same understanding through their merged power. This wasn't destruction wearing the mask of progress, like Williams' work. This was transformation, reality itself recognizing and reaching for its original state. The tear wasn't fighting them; it was trying to help them remember.

Samantha felt blood trickle from her nose as the strain mounted, but she didn't dare break concentration. Through their combined power, she could feel Connor doing complex calculations, adjusting the grid's resonance to match their unified energy.

"Almost," he gritted out. "Just need to—"

A new alarm blared. Rachel's voice cut through the chaos: "Federation ships entering the atmosphere! They're charging weapons!"

Of course they were. The council wouldn't let this continue; they wouldn't let their secrets be exposed. Samantha's mind raced through options as she maintained the containment field. "How long until they're in range?"

"Two minutes," Rachel reported. "Maybe less."

"Not enough time," Connor said. "We need at least five minutes to stabilize the pattern. If they interrupt the process—"

"They'll kill everyone." Samantha made her decision. "Emma!"

Her second's voice came back instantly: "Commander?"

"Get me a channel to those ships. Now."

The connection crackled to life in her ear as she struggled to maintain the containment field. "This is Commander Samantha Reed. Break off your attack and withdraw immediately. We have a critical magical operation in progress. Any interruption will result in catastrophic civilian casualties."

"Commander Reed." The voice that responded was cold and formal. "You are ordered to stand down and withdraw. The council has deemed this situation beyond your authority."

"Beyond my—" She broke off as another surge of power required her attention. "Listen to me. If you interrupt this containment operation, you'll trigger a cascade failure. The entire city—"

"Is already lost. Initiate Protocol Omega. Authorization: Williams, Marcus J."

Samantha's blood ran cold. Protocol Omega—the Federation's final solution. They would rather destroy the city than let the truth be revealed.

"Commander," Emma said urgently. "They're powering up their main guns. Sixty seconds to firing."

Connor's shadows pulsed stronger, taking more of the strain as Samantha split her attention. "Options?"

"Three Federation cruisers," Rachel reported. "Standard shield configuration. If we redirect the grid's energy—"

"We'd lose containment," Connor cut her off. "The cascade would—"

"Wait." Samantha's mind raced through the new mathematics she'd seen in the tear. "The resonance pattern. If we inverse it..."

Connor caught her meaning instantly. "Use their own shield frequencies against them. But that would mean—"

"Trusting each other completely." She met his eyes. "Can you do that?"

His answer was immediate: "Always could. It was you who stopped trusting me."

The words hurt, but there wasn't time to dwell on them. "Emma, Rachel—get everyone to shelter. What we're about to do... just get clear."

As their teams retreated, Samantha took a deep breath. "Ready?"

Connor's shadows merged more fully with her light. "Together."

They moved in perfect synchronization, their combined power flowing through the grid's structure. Samantha felt Connor's calculations mesh with her own as they inverted the resonance pattern. Reality shuddered as they redirected the energy upward toward the attacking ships.

The Federation cruisers didn't realize their danger until too late. Their shields, designed to defend against standard magical attacks, had no defense against the fundamental forces Connor and Samantha wielded together. The resonance pattern shattered their protective fields like glass.

"Break off!" The Federation commander's voice held real fear now. "All ships, emergency withdrawal! Break off!"

But it was too late. The cascade they'd contained below now surged upward, turning the cruisers' own shield frequencies against them. Samantha felt reality twist as the ships' power cores overloaded. They never had a chance to retreat.

The explosion lit up Illyria's sky like a new sun.

When it was over, when the containment field finally stabilized and the tear in reality sealed itself, Samantha found herself still holding Connor's hand. Their combined magic slowly faded, leaving them drained but alive.

And now traitors to the Federation.

"Commander?" Emma approached cautiously, her expression a mix of concern and uncertainty. "What now?"

Samantha looked at the devastation around them, at the teams of rebels and Federation soldiers watching expectantly. At Connor, who had tried to tell her the truth years ago.

"Now," she said quietly, "we find out what else they've been lying about."

The Federation had sent ships to kill them all, to bury the truth along with an entire city. They wouldn't stop coming.

But now she knew why. And that changed everything.

"We'll need somewhere secure," she said to Connor, "somewhere we can plan."

He nodded, understanding everything she wasn't saying. "I know a place. If you're sure about this..."

"I'm sure." She turned to Emma, seeing the question in her second's eyes. "You don't have to come with us. What I'm about to do—"

"Is probably treason," Emma finished. "Little late to worry about that now, isn't it?"

Despite everything, Samantha felt herself smile. "Probably."

They had a lot to figure out: the truth about the Convergence, about what the Federation had done to magic itself, about why they were so desperate to keep it hidden.

But they'd do it together.

The Federation had created her to be their perfect weapon. Time to show them exactly how that decision could backfire.

The real war was just beginning.

SIX

FOUNDATIONS OF FEAR

Marcus Williams stood in his private study, reviewing files that existed nowhere else in Federation space. The weight of family legacy pressed down on him as he activated the most secure privacy shields and called up records that had shaped four generations of institutional control.

The Williams family had been present at every crucial moment in Federation history. His great-grandfather Aldrich had helped design the first frameworks for magical education. His grandfather Thomas had created the bureaucratic structures that governed how magic was taught across Federation space. His father Jonathan had served on the Council that established protocols for containing unified magic.

And Marcus himself had been there for the ultimate expression of that legacy—the choice to break reality itself rather than lose control of it.

But tonight, watching Academy grounds shimmer with temporal distortions through his window, Marcus found himself questioning whether that choice had been heroic or catastrophic.

The complete, unedited records of the Rosewood Incident filled his holographic display—images that still haunted his dreams fifty years later. Where a thriving research colony had once stood, only a dead zone remained. Five hundred square miles of twisted metal and crystallized air where reality itself bore permanent scars.

Marcus had been young then, thirty-four and ambitious, working on practical applications of unified magic. Rosewood had been the Federation's most advanced research facility, staffed by the brightest minds of their generation.

They had been studying natural unified practitioners—individuals who could channel both Luminor and Tenebral energies without technological assistance. The research showed incredible promise, with applications that could revolutionize everything from space travel to planetary engineering.

Dr. Sarah Morgan had been their most gifted subject, a natural unified practitioner whose power levels exceeded anything previously documented. She was also Marcus's closest colleague and research partner.

She was the woman he had loved.

Marcus closed his eyes, allowing himself to remember that final day with perfect, painful clarity. Sarah had arrived at the lab carrying devastating news—her brother David had been killed in a transport accident. A routine supply run had turned tragic when safety protocols failed and the transport's magical containment systems overloaded.

David had been the only qualified engineer on board. He had saved the other passengers, but the effort cost him his life.

"It was preventable," Sarah had said, her voice tight with grief. "The safety systems were outdated, the maintenance ignored, the engineering staff undertrained. David died because the administration chose to save money instead of lives."

Marcus had tried to convince her to take the day off, to process her grief before attempting any complex magical work. But Sarah had been determined to continue.

"David believed in what we're doing here," she had insisted. "He understood that unified magic could solve problems like this—could create safety systems that adapt instead of just following predetermined protocols. The best way to honor his memory is to continue the work."

The cruel irony of those words still burned in Marcus's memory.

The experiment had been routine—a controlled demonstration of unified field manipulation designed to show how natural magic could be safely scaled for industrial applications. Sarah would create a localized energy field while Marcus and the other researchers monitored from the control room.

Initially, everything proceeded perfectly. Sarah's unified magic flowed smoothly, creating precise field effects that were mathematically elegant and completely controlled. The containment systems registered normal stress levels, well within acceptable parameters.

But they hadn't understood the emotional component of unified magic.

Grief was a powerful force, and Sarah had been channeling far more pain than any of them realized. Her conscious control remained perfect, but her unconscious mind was processing trauma in ways that affected her magical output on levels they couldn't monitor.

The first sign of trouble had been subtle—minor fluctuations in the field harmonics that suggested emotional interference.

Marcus had noted the readings with concern but hadn't understood their significance until it was too late.

Sarah's unified magic began responding to her emotional state rather than her conscious intent. The careful field manipulation became something else entirely—a manifestation of grief and rage that fed on itself, growing stronger with each pulse of unconscious emotion.

"Sarah," Marcus had called over the intercom, reading the escalating energy levels with growing alarm. "The emotional resonance is affecting field stability. We need to abort."

She had tried to comply. Marcus could still see her face through the observation window—the concentration as she fought to regain control of power that was slipping beyond conscious direction. But the magic had taken on a life of its own, responding to the depth of pain she had been trying to suppress.

The containment systems failed within minutes. Reality itself began to buckle under the strain of raw emotion given form through unlimited power. The laboratory's instruments registered readings that violated known physics as space-time twisted around Sarah's uncontrolled output.

Marcus had watched helplessly as the woman he loved became a conduit for forces beyond any mortal's ability to contain. Her body began to change, reality reshaping itself around her as unified magic consumed her physical form and transformed her into something that existed partially outside normal space-time.

But the worst part had been her awareness. Even as the transformation progressed, even as her body dissolved into patterns of pure energy, Sarah had remained conscious. She had understood what was happening, had seen the devastation spreading outward from her position.

"Marcus," she had whispered, her voice somehow reaching him across dimensional barriers that her power had torn open. "Stop this. Whatever it takes. Don't let this happen to anyone else."

The evacuation alarms sounded as sections of the facility began existing in multiple dimensions simultaneously. Marcus found himself running through corridors where the laws of physics no longer applied, past laboratories where time moved in circles and space folded back on itself.

Some of his colleagues had been caught in the expanding reality storm. Dr. Peterson was frozen in temporal loops, experiencing the same moment of terror repeatedly. Dr. Kim had been stretched across multiple dimensional states, conscious in all of them but unable to act in any.

And at the center of it all, Sarah continued transforming into something that was no longer entirely human, her consciousness expanding beyond physical boundaries while reality rewrote itself according to the patterns of her unconscious grief.

The end had come without warning. Sarah's expanded awareness finally grasped the full scope of what her uncontrolled power was doing to the people around her. In a final act of conscious will, she had turned her unified magic inward, using it to contain and then collapse her own existence.

The resulting explosion had been visible from orbit. When emergency response teams finally reached the site, they found a crater where the research facility had been, surrounded by a zone where reality itself remained permanently damaged.

Marcus had been among the few survivors, rescued from the facility's outer sections where the reality distortions had been less severe. The medical teams found him in a catatonic state, his mind struggling to process trauma that violated basic assumptions about the nature of existence.

The official reports described equipment failure and experimental overreach. They didn't mention that a single person's loss of emotional control had nearly torn a hole in the fabric of existence itself.

Marcus returned to the present, staring at psychological evaluations from the years following Rosewood. The patterns were clear—traumatic fixation, projection of grief onto institutional policy, the gradual replacement of scientific objectivity with fear-based reasoning.

Dr. Elizabeth Kane, the lead psychological evaluator, had been particularly perceptive: "Subject demonstrates classic symptoms of trauma-based fixation. His obsession with controlling unified magic appears to be a projection of his inability to control the loss of Dr. Morgan. Recommend extended therapy before returning to active research."

Marcus had ignored her recommendations. Instead, he had used his growing influence within Federation hierarchy to ensure that unified magic research would be strictly controlled, that no one else would suffer Sarah's fate or witness the kind of devastation that emotional instability could unleash through unlimited power.

The Williams family legacy had provided him with the political connections necessary to implement his vision. His great-grandfather's warnings about ungovernable magical practitioners became the foundation for new policies. His grandfather's institutional frameworks were expanded to include sophisticated monitoring systems. His father's Council position allowed for the passage of regulations that made natural unified magic effectively illegal.

And Marcus himself had designed the theoretical frameworks that justified it all—mathematical models demonstrating the inherent instability of unified magic, psychological profiles identifying potential risks, institutional protocols channeling magical development into safe, controllable directions.

It had been brilliant work, comprehensive and systematic. It had also been built on a foundation of trauma and fear rather than objective scientific analysis.

Marcus closed the files and walked to his window, looking out at Academy grounds where reality itself had become unstable. Fifty years of careful work, of building institutional frameworks designed to prevent another Rosewood, and he was watching it all crumble.

But perhaps that was inevitable. Perhaps Sarah's final words had carried a different meaning than he'd understood. Perhaps she hadn't been asking him to prevent unified magic from manifest-·ing, but to prevent the kind of institutional constraints that had made her tragedy possible in the first place.

The weight of that possibility settled over him as he prepared for what was to come. The Academy was changing, reality itself was shifting, and soon he would face a choice that would define not just his legacy but the future of magical understanding itself.

Everything his family had built to control unified magic was failing. The question was whether he would go down fighting to maintain that control, or whether he would finally honor Sarah's memory by choosing a different path.

The shadows in his study seemed to whisper her name as he made his decision.

Some battles were worth fighting.

Some were worth losing.

And some were worth walking away from entirely.

The choice would come soon enough.

SEVEN
NEW DIRECTIONS

The rebel base's war room hummed with tension. Maps and tactical displays covered every wall, showing Federation fleet movements and emergency response patterns across Illyria. Samantha's attention fixed on the central holotable, where Connor's grid patterns still pulsed with residual energy.

"The Federation's scrambling everything they have," Emma reported, scanning real-time data feeds. "Three battle groups diverted from outer systems. They won't take chances after losing those cruisers."

"They can't afford to." Connor's shadows had receded, but exhaustion lined his face. "Not with what we could reveal."

Samantha studied the tactical display, her mind processing options. The Federation's response matched her training predictions exactly: overwhelming force with minimal warning. They'd shoot first, destroy evidence, write whatever report suited them.

"We need to move," she decided. "This location's compromised."

Rachel Thompson looked up from her displays. "We have fallback positions, but moving this many people—"

"Will be noticed." Samantha turned to Emma. "The Seraphine's transponder codes—you can replicate them?"

Emma's eyes lit with understanding. "Create multiple signals, split their forces. They'll know it's a trick."

"They'll suspect," Connor corrected. "But they'll have to check each signal. Protocol demands it." His slight smile showed he recognized the irony of using Federation rules against them.

Samantha nodded. "How many ships can you fake?"

"With the rebel comm gear?" Emma exchanged glances with Rachel. "Maybe three convincing signatures. More if we don't need them to hold up to close scanning."

"Do it." Samantha turned to Connor. "Your people—how mobile are they?"

"Most can move immediately. The sensitives will need special transport. The Tenebral exposure makes normal movement... difficult."

The implications hung heavy between them. They'd all seen what prolonged exposure to pure Tenebral energy could do to the unprepared. Even controlled use left its mark.

"I can help with that." Samantha met his eyes. "If we combine our magic again, create a containment field—"

"No." Connor's response was immediate. "We're both still recovering from the grid operation. Another working that size could kill us."

"He's right," Emma added. "Your nose bled for an hour after. Whatever that combined magic does, it takes a toll."

Samantha wanted to argue, but they spoke truth. She could still feel the strain from earlier, the way reality had fought their attempt to merge such fundamentally opposed forces. The

Academy had theories about why, but now she knew the truth—she knew what the Federation had done to magic itself.

Images from their old research journals flashed through her mind. The forbidden texts they'd found buried in theoretical archives spoke of unified beings who could channel both aspects of magic as naturally as breathing. They'd dismissed those accounts as allegory or exaggeration. But their own experiments had started showing similar results—moments when light and shadow moved as one, when the boundaries between magical disciplines blurred into something older, something whole.

She remembered the day they'd merged their magics for the first time, how the resulting patterns had matched exactly with those descriptions. Williams had confiscated their data the next morning, citing regulation violations. But not before they'd seen proof that unification wasn't just possible—it was natural.

"How long do we have?" she asked instead.

Rachel checked her displays. "Based on fleet movements? Six hours before they're in position to lock down the whole sector. Less if they deploy from the capital."

"They will." Samantha's voice was grim. "Williams won't wait for the battle groups. He'll send everything he has locally."

"Williams." Connor's expression darkened. "There's something you should see." He gestured, shadows swirling to life above the holotable. Images formed: classified documents, personnel files, mission reports. "Found these in the restricted archives before I left."

Samantha scanned the documents, her throat tightening. Councilor Marcus Williams appeared in most of them, connected to something called Project Sundering. The dates went back decades.

"He was there," Connor said quietly. "When they broke it. When they split magic itself into Luminor and Tenebral, he helped design the process."

"That's impossible," Emma protested. "The split happened centuries ago. The historical records—"

"Are lies." Samantha's voice turned cold. "Like everything else they taught us." She turned to Connor. "How did you find this?"

"Accident. I was researching unified field theory for an advanced class. Found references that didn't match official records. Started digging." His shadows flickered. "Williams caught me in the archives. Tried to have me eliminated quietly. That's when I ran."

The pieces clicked into place—the assassination attempt that had started Connor's rebellion, the Federation's increasingly desperate attempts to control magic, the Convergence itself.

"It's trying to fix itself," Samantha realized. "Magic. Reality. That's what the Convergence really is. The universe is trying to heal what they broke."

"And now we know why they're so desperate to stop it." Connor's eyes met hers. "Why they'd destroy a city to keep the truth hidden."

The implications staggered her. Everything the Federation had built was based on the artificial separation of magical forces. If that separation ended, if magic became whole again...

Another memory surfaced: their final project in Advanced Theoretical Applications. They'd discovered anomalous resonance patterns in supposedly separate magical fields—patterns that shouldn't exist according to Federation doctrine. Connor had stayed up three nights straight, mapping the mathematical correlations while she refined the practical applications.

"Look at this, Sam," he'd said, eyes bright with discovery. "These equations don't describe two different forces—they're showing the same thing from different angles. Like a crystal fractured and trying to reform." They'd been so close to understanding before Williams had shut down their research line and separated their academic tracks. Now she understood why.

"We need to copy these files," Samantha decided. "All of them. Get them somewhere safe."

"Already done," Connor said. "Multiple copies, hidden caches. Insurance."

He pulled up another set of files, these encoded in layers of shadow magic. "Remember that week we spent analyzing the Restoration Codex? The passages about divided souls finding their way back to wholeness?" The documents flickered with familiar equations—their old research notes, expanded and refined through years of hidden study.

"The Federation didn't just split magic, Sam. They split everything. But look—" His shadows traced complex patterns in the air, patterns she recognized from their Academy days. "Some things can't stay broken forever. The mathematics doesn't lie. What was whole once can be whole again."

The implications made her breath catch. Their old theories about magical resonance hadn't just been academic exercises—they'd been rediscovering fundamental truths about the nature of reality itself. About what was possible when artificial barriers fell away.

"Smart." She turned back to the tactical display. "Emma, start those transponder signals. Rachel, prep your people for evacuation. Non-essential personnel first, then the sensitives. We'll split into three groups—harder to track, better chances of some getting through."

"Where are we going?" Emma asked.

Samantha studied the star charts, considering options. They needed somewhere defensible, somewhere with access to both magical and technical resources, somewhere the Federation wouldn't expect.

"The Academy," she said finally.

Connor stiffened. "That's suicide. It's the most heavily defended facility in the sector."

"Exactly why they won't expect us to go there." Samantha allowed herself a small smile. "Besides, you still have access to the sealed archives. Don't you?"

He matched her smile. "Maybe."

"Wait," Emma interrupted. "The Academy? That's—"

"Where everything started," Samantha finished. "Where they've been training people to use broken magic for generations. If we want answers, if we want proof we can show others..." She gestured to the tactical display. "We need access to those archives. The real ones."

"It's also where they keep the original research," Connor added. "Project Sundering. Everything about what they did to magic itself."

Understanding dawned in Emma's eyes. "We're not just running. We're gathering evidence."

"More than that." Samantha's voice hardened. "We're going to show everyone what the Federation really is, what they did to reality itself." She looked at Connor. "Together."

He nodded slowly. "Together."

The war room burst into activity as they began evacuation preparations. But Samantha's mind was already at the Academy, remembering corridors she'd walked as a student—corridors that held secrets she'd never suspected.

The Federation had built its power on broken magic and buried truth. Time to dig it all up.

"Commander?" Emma's voice pulled her back to the present. "There's something else. When we were containing the grid energy... I saw something in the tear. Something about the original Sundering."

Samantha felt Connor's attention sharpen. "What did you see?"

Emma hesitated. "Not saw, exactly. More like... felt. Like the memory was written into reality itself." She shuddered. "They didn't just split magic. They had to split everything. Reality, time, space... even people."

The implications hit Samantha like a physical blow. She looked at Connor and saw the same realization in his eyes.

Their connection. The way their magic worked together. The reason the Federation had been so desperate to keep them apart.

"We need to move," she said quietly. "Now."

The Federation hadn't just broken magic—they'd broken everything.

And the Convergence was coming to put it all back together.

Ready or not.

EIGHT
BREAKING FORMATION

The evacuation was going too smoothly. Samantha knew better than to trust easy operations—something always broke, usually at the worst possible moment.

But this felt different. Through their unified magic, she and Connor could sense the Convergence's patterns shifting around them. Where Williams' experiments left reality cracked and bleeding, the Convergence moved like water seeking its natural course. Even now, she could see how it flowed around their combined power, not fighting but harmonizing as if recognizing something it had been seeking.

She remembered texts from the restricted archives—accounts of the First Convergence when reality had briefly remembered its original state. The Federation had recorded it as a catastrophic breakdown, but watching the patterns now, she saw what those writers had meant. This wasn't destruction. It was reality trying to heal itself.

She stood in the rebel base's main hangar, watching teams load equipment and personnel into transport ships. Emma's false transponder signals were already active, drawing Federation pursuit forces in three different directions. But they couldn't count on that distraction lasting long.

"Last of the sensitives are loaded," Rachel reported, approaching with a data tablet. "Medical teams say the containment fields are holding, but—"

The entire base shuddered. Warning klaxons blared as emergency lights flashed to life.

"There it is," Samantha muttered. "Report!"

"Federation advance forces," Connor called from the tactical station. "Three strike teams, moving fast. They're not waiting for the battle groups."

Of course they weren't. Williams would have hand-picked teams —people who could move instantly, who wouldn't ask questions about killing their own.

"Time to primary defensive line?" Samantha asked.

"Four minutes. Maybe less."

Not enough time to get everyone out. They needed at least fifteen minutes to clear the hangar and get their ships past the atmosphere. She looked at Connor and saw him reach the same conclusion.

"We'll hold them," he said.

Emma stepped forward. "Commander, you can't—"

"Get these ships in the air," Samantha ordered. "Full evacuation protocols. We'll delay the strike teams."

"Sam." Emma's voice dropped. "You know what those teams are capable of. Even together—"

"We don't have a choice." Samantha checked her weapons and

felt the familiar hum of stored magic. "They catch us boxed in here, it's over."

Rachel's shadows flickered. "My team can—"

"No." Connor's voice was firm. "Get your people out. The sensitives need protection more than we do."

Samantha noted his use of "we" with distant amusement. Two days ago, they'd been trying to kill each other. Now, they were planning a last stand together.

Through their merged consciousness, they felt how their unified magic rippled outward, touching other pairs throughout the base—rebels and Federation soldiers whose powers had started resonating in unexpected ways. Like their own connection, these harmonies weren't forcing anything new; they were revealing something that had always existed. Each unified pair created patterns that echoed the Convergence's own rhythm.

The Federation taught that such combinations would tear reality apart. But watching these natural unifications bloom amid the chaos, Samantha understood the truth. Reality wasn't breaking—it was remembering. Just as she and Connor had remembered, just as others were beginning to remember. The artificial barriers were falling away, revealing what had always been whole.

The universe had an interesting sense of humor.

"Three minutes," Connor reported. "They're moving in standard Federation assault pattern."

"Of course they are." Samantha smiled grimly. "Because Williams thinks we'll counter with standard rebel tactics."

Connor matched her smile. "Shall we disappoint him?"

They moved together toward the hangar entrance, their magic already beginning to merge. Golden light met shadow as they prepared defensive positions, working with the easy synchronization of long practice.

The spaces their unified magic touched responded differently than either had seen before. Instead of forcing reality to bend, their combined power seemed to reveal underlying patterns that had always been there—like dust falling away from a mosaic. Where artificial unification left scars in space-time, their natural unity activated something dormant in reality's fabric.

Connor's shadows traced the mathematical frameworks taking shape around them. "These aren't random fluctuations," he said. "The Convergence is following the same resonance patterns we discovered in our Academy research—the ones that suggested magic was originally one force." Their unified magic wasn't fighting the Convergence; it was speaking the same language.

"Remember advanced tactical?" Connor asked as they worked. "The simulations we used to run?"

"You always tried to overcomplicate them." Samantha channeled power into the hangar's structural supports, strengthening them against what was coming. "Three-layer defense when one would do."

"And you always went for the direct approach." His shadows spread through the hangar, creating zones of twisted space. "Even when subtlety would work better."

"Look who's talking about subtlety." But she was smiling as she said it.

Behind them, ships began lifting off. Emma and Rachel coordinated the evacuation with efficient precision, getting their people out in precise waves. Every second they bought increased the chances of escape.

The base shook again. Closer this time.

"Two minutes," Connor reported. "They're—" He broke off, eyes widening. "That's not possible."

"What?"

"These energy readings. The strike teams... Sam, they're using combined magic."

Samantha's blood ran cold. "Show me."

The tactical display told the story. The Federation teams were somehow wielding both Luminor and Tenebral energy together —not as smoothly as she and Connor could, but enough to be lethal.

"Williams," she breathed. "He's been experimenting, testing ways to control unified magic."

"Using his own people as test subjects." Connor's shadows darkened with anger. "That's why the Convergence is accelerating. Their experiments are destabilizing the natural balance."

Another impact rattled the base. Warning indicators flashed as outer defenses began to fail.

"One minute," Connor said quietly.

Samantha made a decision. "Emma! New plan. Get everyone out now. Emergency protocols."

"But the loading sequence—"

"Forget the sequence. Just go. Now."

Emma hesitated for only an instant before nodding sharply. Ships began lifting off in ragged waves, pilots pushing their engines dangerously. But they were moving.

"Rachel," Connor called. "Make sure the sensitives' ship gets priority. Keep them safe."

Rachel's expression said she wanted to argue, but she complied. Within moments, the hangar was nearly empty except for their remaining defensive teams.

"Thirty seconds," Connor reported.

Samantha turned to the defenders. "Fall back to the ships. That's an order."

They began retreating, though she saw the reluctance in their eyes. These people—both rebel and Federation—had chosen to stay when the truth came out, had chosen to follow her and Connor into whatever came next.

She wouldn't waste their loyalty.

"Ready?" she asked Connor as the last defenders reached their ships.

He nodded, shadows swirling faster around him. "Just like the old days."

"The old days didn't have strike teams using unified magic."

"True." His smile was fierce. "This should be interesting."

The first blast hit the hangar entrance like a hammer. Combined magic shattered their outer defenses, sending fragments of metal and energy scattering across the floor. Through the breach, Samantha saw Federation strike teams advancing. Their armor crackled with impossible energies as both light and shadow answered their commands.

It should have been beautiful. Instead, it was horrifying. She could see the strain it put on them, the way reality itself rebelled against this forced joining of powers. Williams hadn't figured out how to safely combine the magics. He was burning his own people out to achieve it.

"Pattern Sigma," she said to Connor, "like in the simulations."

He nodded, understanding immediately. Their magic merged smoothly as thought, golden light and shadow weaving together in perfect harmony. This was how it was supposed to work. Natural. Unified.

The strike teams hit their first defensive line like a battering ram. Combined magic met combined magic in a spectacular display of power. But where the Federation teams fought against their abilities and struggled to control the unified force, Samantha and Connor worked as one.

Their counter-attack sent the first wave staggering back. Reality twisted as Connor's shadows created zones of impossible geometry, while Samantha's light formed precise mathematical patterns to channel the chaos. Working together, they forced the strike teams to retreat and regroup.

But it couldn't last. Already, she felt the strain of sustained unified magic use, and she saw Connor's shadows flickering as he fought to maintain control.

"Ships are away," Emma's voice came through their comms. "Only your exit craft remaining. Get out of there!"

"Time to go," Connor said, his voice tight with effort.

Samantha nodded. Together, they began falling back toward their waiting ship. But as they retreated, she saw something that made her pause.

One of the strike team members was moving wrong, fighting against his own actions. His magic flickered erratically as if...

"They're being controlled," she realized. "Williams isn't just experimenting on them. He's forcing them to use the unified magic, overriding their will somehow."

Connor saw it too. His expression hardened as he reached out with his shadows, trying to break whatever hold Williams had on the soldiers. But the control was too deep, too fundamental.

"We can't help them," he said quietly. "Not yet. Not without understanding how he's doing it."

Another wave of attacks forced them back. Their ship waited, engines hot, ready for immediate departure. But Samantha's mind was racing with implications.

If Williams could control his soldiers this completely, what else was he capable of? What other experiments had he been running in secret?

"Sam!" Connor's warning came just in time.

She threw up a barrier as a massive surge of unified magic threatened to overwhelm them. The strike teams were pressing harder, ignoring their own injuries, their own obvious pain like puppets on strings.

They reached their ship as the hangar began to collapse. Connor's shadows cut off pursuit while Samantha's light sealed the hull breaches their retreat had caused. Within moments, they were airborne.

"Multiple pursuit craft launching," Emma reported from the tactical station. "They're not giving up."

"Of course not." Samantha strapped into the command chair. "Williams can't let us reach the Academy and access those records."

"About that." Connor's voice was tight as he worked the ship's defensive systems. "There's something else in those files, something about why unified magic works so naturally for us."

"Tell me."

"Later. When we're not about to die."

Fair point. Samantha turned her attention to flying, to keeping them alive long enough to learn the truth. But his words nagged at her.

Why did their magic work so well together? What was the connection that let them unify their powers so naturally when others burned themselves out trying?

The answers waited in the Academy's archives—assuming they lived long enough to reach them.

"Hold on," she warned as pursuit ships opened fire. "This is going to get interesting."

Their ship dove into Illyria's atmosphere, into the storm of fire and magic that waited. Behind them, the rebel base collapsed in on itself, burying its secrets.

But the biggest secrets were still to come.

And the Federation would do anything to keep them hidden.

NINE
PURSUIT COURSE

The cosmos twisted around their ship as Samantha pushed its magical engines to their limit. Behind them, Federation pursuit craft maintained formation with mechanical precision, their weapons spitting lines of combined energy through the void.

"Shields at sixty percent," Emma reported from tactical. "That last hit nearly breached the starboard containment grid."

Connor's shadows danced across the defensive displays, reinforcing weak points. "They're not trying to destroy us. The pattern suggests they want us disabled, captured."

"Of course they do." Samantha executed a tight spiral, dodging another burst of unified magic. "Williams wants to know how we're combining powers so effectively. Probably wants to dissect us to find out."

"Charming thought." Connor's voice was dry. "Three more ships joining the pursuit. Reading heavy magical signatures."

Samantha checked the tactical display. The new ships were

larger and heavier-armed—not the standard pursuit craft they'd been facing. These were something else.

"Those are Academy ships," she realized, "advanced tactical training vessels. Williams isn't just sending strike teams."

"He's sending teachers," Connor finished. His expression darkened. "The ones who helped him experiment on students."

The implications chilled her. How long had the Academy been involved? In how many "training accidents" had Williams actually been testing his theories about unified magic?

No time to dwell on it. The Academy ships were moving to cut off their escape vectors, herding them away from their planned route. Standard containment tactics, executed with practiced skill.

"Options?" Emma asked.

Samantha studied the tactical display, mind racing through scenarios. The Academy ships would know all the standard evasion patterns and would be ready for any normal escape attempt.

Time to be abnormal.

"Connor." She met his eyes. "Remember that simulation you designed? The one they banned after first testing?"

His shadows flickered with understanding. "The phase-shift maneuver? That was theoretical. We never actually—"

"Because they shut down the program before we could try." She smiled grimly. "No better time to test a theory."

"Wait," Emma cut in. "What exactly are we talking about?"

"Using unified magic to briefly shift our ship out of normal space-time," Connor explained, "creating a quantum tunnel through the pursuit formation."

Emma's eyes widened. "That's impossible. The energy requirements alone—"

"Would burn out normal mages," Samantha finished. "But we're not normal mages. And we don't have much choice."

Another hit rocked the ship. "Shields at forty percent," Emma reported. "We try something like that with the containment grid already damaged..."

She left the thought unfinished. They all knew the risks. One mistake with unified magic at these energy levels would tear their ship apart.

"Alternative suggestions welcome," Samantha said, executing another evasive pattern.

Emma studied her tactical displays. "We could try to reach the nearest shipping lane. Use the commercial traffic for cover."

"Too far," Connor said. "They'd catch us before we got halfway there." His shadows spread across the bridge displays, analyzing pursuit patterns. "The phase shift is risky, but it's our best chance."

Samantha nodded. "Emma, divert all non-essential power to the containment grid. We'll only get one shot at this."

As Emma worked, Samantha exchanged looks with Connor. They'd designed this maneuver years ago when they were still students pushing the boundaries of magical theory, before the Federation had shut down their research, before everything had fallen apart.

"Ready?" she asked.

Connor moved to the auxiliary control station, shadows merging with the ship's systems. "Like old times."

"Better hope not. Most of our old experiments exploded."

His laugh was genuine. "Only the interesting ones."

The Academy ships were closing fast, their formation perfect for standard containment. Too perfect. They didn't expect anything outside normal tactical doctrine.

Time to show them why the Federation had been so afraid of their research.

"Emma," Samantha called, "plot us a course directly through their formation. Center mass."

"Through—" Emma's protest cut off as understanding dawned. "Right. Course plotted. You're either brilliant or insane."

"Probably both," Connor offered.

Samantha reached for her magic, feeling Connor do the same. Golden light met shadow as their power merged, flowing into the ship's systems. The containment grid hummed as unified magic filled it, reality itself beginning to bend around their hull.

"Energy spike detected," Emma reported. "They're reading our power buildup. Academy ships moving to intercept."

"Let them come," Samantha said quietly. "Containment status?"

"Holding. Barely." Emma's fingers flew across her controls. "Whatever you're going to do, do it fast."

The Academy ships opened fire, their weapons charged with unified magic of their own. But their attacks felt wrong—forced, artificial. They were using technology to combine magical forces that were never meant to be mechanically merged.

"Now," Samantha said.

She and Connor moved in perfect sync, their unified magic surging through the ship's systems. Reality shuddered as they tore a hole in space-time itself, creating a tunnel of possibility through normal space.

The sensation was indescribable. For a moment that lasted both an instant and an eternity, they existed everywhere and nowhere. Their unified magic moved through space-time like water finding its natural course. Where the Federation ships' artificial unification left reality scarred and twisted, their combined power seemed to heal the fabric of space as they passed through it. The phase shift wasn't forcing reality to change—it was asking reality to remember its original state.

Through their merged consciousness, they felt other pairs of mages throughout both fleets responding to their passage—powers resonating in ways that made the Federation's forced unity seem crude by comparison. Natural harmonies were awakening, like instruments finding their true tune after centuries of enforced discord.

Samantha felt Connor's presence like a lifeline, their combined power holding the ship together as they phased through dimensions.

Then they were through, emerging behind the pursuit formation.

"Holy hell," Emma breathed. "You actually did it."

The Academy ships scrambled to react, their perfect formation shattered. But by the time they brought weapons to bear, Samantha had already pushed their engines to maximum burn.

"Pursuit craft attempting to match course," Emma reported. "But that phase shift disrupted their targeting systems. We've got a clear run."

Samantha nodded, but her attention was on Connor. His shadows had retreated, and she saw blood trickling from his nose. The unified magic had taken its toll on both of them.

"Status?" she asked quietly.

"I'll live." He wiped the blood away. "That was... different than the simulations."

"Everything's different now." She checked their course and confirmed they were back on track for the Academy. "Think they'll expect us to try something like that again?"

"Williams will." Connor's expression was thoughtful. "He always said we were his most promising students. Now we know why."

"Because we can unify magic naturally?"

"Because we were already unified." He met her eyes. "That's what I found in the archives. About the Sundering, about why they split magic apart. They didn't just separate magical forces—they separated people. Souls."

The implications hit her like a physical blow. "We're..."

"Connected. Always have been. The Sundering split us apart before we were born, but it couldn't completely break the connection. That's why our magic works together so naturally."

"That's why Williams was so interested in our research," Samantha realized. "We weren't just theorizing about unified magic. We were unconsciously remembering how it used to work."

"And now the Convergence is trying to put everything back together." Connor's shadows flickered. "Including us."

The truth settled over them like a weight. They'd been drawn together at the Academy, pushed apart by Federation lies, and now reunited by the very force they'd been taught to fear.

"Commander," Emma's voice cut through the moment. "Long-range sensors are picking up something ahead. Some kind of disturbance around the Academy."

Samantha checked the readings and felt that Connor did the same. The space around their destination writhed with unified magic as if reality itself was thin there.

"The Convergence," Connor said quietly. "It's affecting the Academy more strongly than anywhere else."

"Because that's where the Sundering began," Samantha finished, "where they first split magic apart."

And that's where they had to go to find the truth, to understand what had been done to them—to everyone.

"Plot an approach vector," she ordered. "But be ready for anything. Something tells me getting in won't be as hard as dealing with what we find inside."

The Academy loomed larger in their viewport, its prestigious towers now resembling prison walls. Somewhere in those halls were the answers they searched for about their true identities and what had been taken from them. It was time to take it back.

All of it.

TEN
FOUNDATIONS CRACKING

Emma Carter had built her entire career on understanding how organizations functioned. Seven years as a Federation communications officer had taught her to read the patterns behind official procedures, to recognize when administrative actions served purposes beyond their stated goals.

Which made what she was discovering in the tactical databases all the more troubling.

She sat in the Seraphine's auxiliary research station, surrounded by communication logs that refused to make sense according to everything she'd been taught about Federation protocols. Her hands moved across the control interfaces, cross-referencing data streams she'd never thought to analyze together before.

The patterns were subtle but unmistakable once you knew what to look for.

Connor Blake's rebellion hadn't emerged in isolation. Emma's communication analysis revealed a network of coordinated administrative actions spanning multiple Academy facilities across Federation space. Not random personnel decisions, but a systematic program of identification and removal.

"Computer, display inter-facility communication logs for the past fifteen years, Academy administrative channels only."

The data that populated her screens painted a picture that made her stomach tighten. Coded communications between Academy administrators, using bureaucratic language that seemed routine on the surface but revealed deeper coordination when analyzed for patterns.

"Subject exhibits concerning theoretical orientations"—repeated across dozens of facilities.

"Recommend administrative reassignment to outer sector monitoring"—a phrase that appeared in conjunction with specific student profiles.

"Special processing protocols initiated"—always followed by communication blackouts regarding those individuals.

Emma's background in tactical communications gave her insights that pure researchers would miss. She recognized the hallmarks of coordinated information suppression: standardized language, synchronized timing, and most telling of all, communication gaps where official records should exist.

This wasn't academic administration. This was intelligence operation methodology applied to educational institutions.

"Computer, cross-reference communication patterns with Academy budget allocations, psychological evaluation departments."

The results confirmed her worst suspicions. Funding for "student wellness programs" had increased dramatically over the past decade, but the money wasn't going to counseling or support services. It was funding specialized facilities, advanced medical equipment, and personnel with backgrounds in memory therapy and consciousness modification.

The Federation wasn't just monitoring problematic students—they were running a sophisticated program to identify, process, and either redirect or eliminate individuals who discovered inconvenient truths.

Emma pulled up her personal authorization codes and accessed the communication archives she normally managed for tactical operations. Her clearance level gave her access to operational protocols that most Academy staff never saw.

What she found there made her hands shake.

"Project Threshold"—a multi-Academy initiative for "managing theoretical divergence in advanced magical education." The documentation was carefully clinical, describing systematic procedures for identifying students whose research approached "security-sensitive theoretical boundaries."

The project had three phases: Identification, Evaluation, and Resolution.

Identification involved monitoring student research through embedded observation protocols and flagging theoretical work that approached forbidden areas. Evaluation assessed whether students could be redirected to acceptable research paths. Resolution... Resolution had multiple subcategories, including "administrative reassignment," "memory modification therapy," and "permanent removal from program."

Emma's tactical training helped her read between the bureaucratic language. Permanent removal didn't mean expulsion. It meant disappearance.

"Computer, analyze communication frequency patterns between Academy facilities and outer sector assignments."

The data revealed something that turned her blood cold. Students "reassigned" to outer sector monitoring showed statistical clustering in the most dangerous, remote, and statistically fatal assignments available. Mining operations with high casualty rates. Frontier research with minimal backup protocols. Deep space exploration with minimal return probability.

They weren't reassigning problematic students. They were killing them through administrative procedure.

Emma's communication expertise let her trace the administrative pathways that made this possible. Carefully crafted transfer orders that looked routine but placed individuals in maximum danger. Communication protocols that ensured these transfers bypassed normal safety reviews. Record-keeping procedures that made tracking long-term outcomes difficult.

The entire system was designed with plausible deniability built into every layer.

Her secure communication terminal chimed with an incoming message. Marcus Kellerman, her old Academy friend who now worked in the Federation archives.

"Emma," his message began, "I ran those searches you requested. You need to be careful. Very careful. What you're looking for... people have disappeared for asking these questions. The communication logs show patterns of surveillance activation whenever certain search parameters are used."

He'd attached a data package with additional findings. Emma opened it with growing dread.

"Administrative Procedure 847-C: Monitoring and Response Protocols for Information Security Breaches," the first document was titled. It detailed surveillance procedures for Academy personnel who accessed restricted research databases, including automated flagging systems that triggered investigation protocols.

Emma realized with dawning horror that her own searches might have already triggered those systems. Her communication access, her pattern analysis, her cross-referencing of databases—all of it could be monitored and flagged as suspicious activity.

But there was more. Kellerman had found evidence of a broader network than just the Academy. Federation communication logs showed similar patterns across military installations, research facilities, and civilian administrative centers. Project Threshold wasn't limited to magical education—it was a civilization-wide program for managing information security.

"Computer, analyze my personal access logs for the past week."

The results confirmed her fears. Her search patterns had indeed triggered monitoring protocols. Security subroutines were already analyzing her activities, cross-referencing her queries with threat assessment databases.

She had hours, maybe less, before her investigations would be classified as a security risk.

Emma's tactical mind shifted into operational mode. She began copying critical data to encrypted storage devices, preparing multiple backup protocols for the information she'd gathered. If she was going to be eliminated or "reassigned," at least the evidence might survive.

As she worked, another piece of the puzzle fell into place. Commander Reed's mission to eliminate Connor Blake wasn't just about stopping a rebel threat. It was about silencing someone who'd escaped the Threshold protocols, someone who retained knowledge the Federation couldn't afford to have spread.

Blake's rebellion wasn't the cause of his elimination order—it was the excuse.

Emma's hands moved quickly across the communication interfaces, sending encrypted copies of her findings to secure locations outside Federation monitoring. The evidence needed to survive even if she didn't.

A priority message flashed on her tactical display. "Emergency recall to Central Command for debriefing and reassignment. Report immediately upon return from current mission."

The administrative language was polite and routine. But Emma's communication training let her recognize the subtextual patterns. This wasn't a routine reassignment—it was a Threshold Resolution order disguised as normal procedure.

She was already marked for elimination.

Emma stood and gathered her encrypted data devices, her mind racing through options. Commander Reed needed to know what they were really fighting, what the Federation actually was beneath its facade of order and justice.

But first, she had to survive long enough to deliver the warning.

The tactical communication station chimed again with another message, this time from Federation Internal Security: "Officer Carter, please confirm your current status and estimated return time. Your presence is required for immediate consultation on communication protocols."

They were closing in. The administrative machinery was already moving to contain her, just as it had contained countless others who'd discovered too much.

Emma deleted her search histories and activated secure erasure protocols for her workstation. Whatever happened next, the Federation wouldn't get the satisfaction of learning exactly how much she'd discovered or how she'd done it.

She walked toward Commander Reed's quarters, carrying the weight of institutional betrayal and the knowledge that the organization she'd served her entire adult life was built on systematic suppression of truth.

The foundation wasn't just cracking around her. It was actively hunting those who noticed the cracks.

And now she was one of them.

Her only hope was that Commander Reed would prove more loyal to truth than to the institution that had shaped them both. Because Emma was about to ask her to choose between comfortable lies and dangerous reality.

The choice that would determine not just their individual fates, but whether anyone would survive to expose what the Federation had become.

Time was running out. For all of them.

ELEVEN
ECHOES OF TRUTH

Samantha looked up from her personal files as Emma entered her quarters, her second's expression grim and urgent. Something in Emma's bearing made Samantha immediately close her research into the Academy records.

"Commander, we need to talk. Now." Emma activated the room's privacy shields and pulled out an encrypted data device. "What I'm about to show you changes everything about this mission."

Samantha gestured to the chair across from her desk. "Show me."

Emma's hands moved quickly across the holographic display, bringing up communication logs and administrative patterns. "Project Threshold. It's a Federation-wide program for eliminating people who discover inconvenient truths. Connor Blake isn't a rebel who went rogue—he's someone who escaped systematic elimination."

The data painted a picture that connected directly to Samantha's own discoveries. While she'd found evidence of personal memory modification, Emma had uncovered the entire institutional machinery that made such operations possible.

"These communication patterns show coordination across dozens of Academy facilities," Emma continued, her voice tight. "Students who approach 'security-sensitive theoretical boundaries' get flagged for resolution. That resolution includes memory modification, dangerous reassignments, or worse."

Samantha studied the administrative protocols Emma had discovered. "The same system that modified my memories."

"Your memories?" Emma's eyes widened. "Commander, what did you find?"

Samantha shared her discoveries about the three-day gap in her Academy schedule, the clinical notation about "special administrative processing," and her growing certainty that crucial memories of her work with Connor had been stolen.

Emma's face went pale. "Then you understand. The Federation isn't fighting chaos—it's maintaining control through information suppression. And now they know I've discovered it."

She showed Samantha the recall orders, the patterns indicating surveillance activation, the administrative language that masked elimination protocols.

"They're moving to eliminate me the same way they've eliminated countless others," Emma said. "I have hours at most before I'm 'reassigned' to a fatal posting."

Samantha leaned back in her chair, processing the implications. Emma's systematic analysis confirmed and expanded on her personal discoveries. The Federation had stolen her memories and was now hunting her second for uncovering the truth.

"Options?" she asked.

"We could abort the mission, try to disappear," Emma said. "But Blake is still out there, and the reality distortions are getting worse. If he really is trying to restore what was taken from us..."

"Then completing this mission might be our best chance of learning the whole truth." Samantha stood and moved to her weapons locker. "But not the way the Federation intended."

Emma's relief was visible. "You believe me?"

"Everything you've found confirms what I suspected about my own situation." Samantha checked her sidearm and sealed the encrypted files they'd both gathered. "The question is whether we're willing to bet our lives that Connor Blake has answers we need."

"The alternative is letting the Federation bury the truth forever," Emma said. "Along with anyone who knows it."

Samantha nodded grimly. "Then we continue to Illyria. But Emma—we go in knowing we might not be coming back to the Federation as the officers we were when we left."

"Understood, Commander."

"And Emma? From this point forward, question everything. Every order, every protocol, every comfortable certainty we've been taught. The Federation we served might not be the organization we thought it was."

They secured their research and prepared to return to the bridge. The mission would continue, but with very different objectives than the Federation intended.

The Academy hadn't changed, but reality had. As their ship approached the massive installation, Samantha saw familiar towers twisted by waves of unified magic. The prestigious halls where she'd trained now rippled with impossible geometries as if the Convergence itself was trying to reshape them.

"Main landing bays are distorted," Emma reported from tactical. "Spatial readings don't make sense. It's like the space inside is... folded."

"The Convergence is stronger here," Connor said, his shadows probing the anomalies. "The original Sundering created weak points in reality. Now they're breaking down."

Samantha studied the readings, remembering corridors she'd walked countless times. "There. Emergency landing pad seven. It's partially shielded from the effects."

"The old maintenance access?" Connor's smile held dark humor. "Where we used to sneak out for unauthorized experiments?"

"Seemed appropriate." She adjusted their approach vector, then glanced at Emma. Her second's expression showed the weight of their new understanding. They were no longer Federation officers following orders. They were individuals seeking truth, regardless of where it led.

"Emma, status of Federation pursuit?"

"Still no signs. Whatever that phase shift did, it threw them off our trail. For now."

They landed without incident, though reality shimmered around them like heat waves. Up close, the distortions were even more pronounced. Parts of the Academy seemed to exist in multiple spaces simultaneously, while others flickered in and out of normal space-time.

"This is wrong," Emma said as they prepared to disembark. "The Convergence shouldn't be this strong yet. According to all our calculations—"

"The calculations assumed natural progression." Connor checked his weapons while his shadows tested the air. "But Williams has been experimenting with unified magic here for years. He's accelerated the process."

"Weakening the barriers between realities," Samantha added.

"Making it easier for the Convergence to break through." She turned to Emma. "Stay with the ship. If anything goes wrong—"

"I'm coming with you." Emma's tone left no room for argument. "You'll need someone watching your backs while you deal with... whatever this is."

She had a point. Samantha and Connor would focus on navigating the distortions of reality, using their unified magic to stay alive. They needed someone to handle more mundane threats.

"Remember the layout?" Samantha asked Connor as they approached the maintenance access.

"Every corridor." His expression darkened. "Including the ones they didn't want us to know about."

The door opened at their approach, reality twisting around the frame. Inside, familiar Academy halls stretched into impossible distances. Light bent wrongly, shadows moved without source, and the very air felt charged with potential.

"The archives are in the central tower," Connor said. "But with these distortions..."

"The direct route might not be direct anymore." Samantha reached out with her magic, feeling Connor do the same. Their unified power touched the distorted space, testing its boundaries.

Images flashed through her mind: corridors she'd never walked, memories that felt both foreign and familiar. She saw herself and Connor in an Academy that never was, practicing magic that had been forbidden for centuries.

"You feel it too?" Connor asked quietly.

She nodded. "Echoes. From before the Sundering."

"From when we were unified."

Emma's sharp breath reminded them they weren't alone. They'd have to explain everything later, but for now...

"This way," Samantha said, following the echo memories. "The distortions are creating paths between spaces that used to be connected, before they split everything apart."

They moved carefully through twisted corridors, using unified magic to stabilize reality around them. The Academy had become a maze of broken space-time, where a single wrong step could leave them trapped between dimensions.

"Wait." Connor held up a hand as they approached a junction. "Look."

Through the reality distortions, they saw figures moving—academy staff, going about their duties as if nothing was wrong. But their movements were wrong, stuttering between moments of time.

"They're caught in temporal flux," Samantha realized. "The Convergence is affecting their perception of time itself."

"Can we help them?" Emma asked.

Connor shook his head. "Not yet. Not until we understand what was done to them—to all of us."

They skirted the temporal anomaly, staying close to walls that occasionally ceased to exist. Samantha felt memories pressing against her consciousness—teaching sessions that never happened, experiments that had been forbidden, moments with Connor that had been stolen from them.

"The archives should be through here," she said, approaching a door that cycled through multiple versions of itself. "If we can stabilize the space long enough to—"

Reality screamed.

The corridor twisted impossibly as a massive surge of unified magic tore through the Academy. Samantha and Connor moved instantly, their power merging to create a bubble of stable space around their group.

"What was that?" Emma demanded, weapon ready.

"Williams." Connor's shadows writhed. "He's trying to control the Convergence effects, force them into patterns he can use."

Through nearby windows, they saw the Academy grounds shifting. Buildings rose and fell, and time accelerated and reversed as Williams attempted to impose his will on reality itself.

"He's making it worse," Samantha said. "The more he fights it, the faster everything breaks down." She turned to Connor. "How long?"

"Before total collapse? Hours maybe. Less if he keeps pushing."

They needed to reach the archives. They needed to find proof of what had been done and understand how to undo it properly. But the surge had changed the layout of reality around them. The direct path was gone.

"There's another way," Connor said. "Through the old testing chambers. The ones they sealed off after..."

After they'd started questioning things. After they'd begun pushing boundaries that threatened Federation control.

"They'll be heavily warded," Samantha pointed out.

"They were warded against separate magics." Connor's shadows curled around his fingers. "Not unified power."

It was risky. The testing chambers had been dangerous even before reality started breaking down. But they were running out of options.

"Lead the way."

They turned down a corridor that shouldn't have existed, following memories that felt more real with each step. Around them, the Academy continued to twist and change as Williams fought against the natural flow of the Convergence.

"Commander." Emma's voice was tight. "These readings... the temporal fluctuations are increasing. If reality breaks down completely—"

"It won't," Samantha said firmly. "Because we're going to fix what they broke. Put everything back together the right way."

"Including us?" Connor asked quietly.

She met his eyes, feeling the echo of connection between them. "Everything."

The truth emerged in fragments: a half-burned document showing original unified formulas, security footage of early experiments, and medical records clinically detailing 'failed separations.' Each piece revealed how thoroughly the Federation had rewritten not just history but reality itself. The deeper they dug, the more evidence they found of a systematic campaign to erase any knowledge of what magic had once been.

The testing chamber entrance appeared ahead—or perhaps had always been there, waiting for them to remember it. Reality rippled around the sealed doors as if even the Convergence was afraid of what lay behind them.

"Ready?" Connor asked, shadows gathering.

Samantha called her power, golden light meeting shadow as they prepared to breach the wards. "Together."

The doors opened, revealing a space that existed in multiple times simultaneously. And in every version, the truth waited to be found.

Time to remember what had been forgotten.

All of it.

TWELVE
REMEMBERED TRUTHS

The testing chamber existed in multiple states simultaneously. Samantha saw it as it had been during their training, as it was now under the Convergence's influence, and as it might have been if the Sundering had never happened. The overlapping realities made her head swim, but something about it felt familiar.

In one temporal stream, she glimpsed records: the Chronicles of the Unified Age, when magic flowed as one force through paired practitioners. The texts spoke of the Resonant Ones—souls naturally drawn together across any distance or barrier. The Federation had dismissed these accounts as myths, but she recognized the patterns they described. They were the same ones she and Connor created naturally, the same ones appearing now throughout the Academy as reality began remembering its true nature.

"Look." Connor pointed to the chamber's center, where reality rippled most strongly. "The temporal nexus is still active."

"After all these years?" Emma raised her weapon as shadows writhed across the walls. "Why would they keep it running?"

"Because they had to." Samantha approached the nexus carefully, feeling its pull on her magic. "This is where they did it, where they first split magic apart."

The chamber had been their favorite testing ground during Academy days. They'd spent countless hours here, pushing the boundaries of what magic could do. But now she understood—they'd been drawn to this place because part of them remembered what had been done here.

"Sam." Connor's voice was tight. "The readings..."

She saw it too. The nexus wasn't just active; it was cycling through moments in time, including the moment of the original Sundering.

"Can we access it?" Emma asked. "See what really happened?"

"Better—" Connor's shadows reached for the nexus "—we can remember it."

Samantha moved to join him, their unified magic merging with the temporal energies. The chamber shuddered as past and present collided.

And they remembered.

The chamber looked different centuries ago, filled with Federation scientists and humming equipment. At its center stood the original temporal nexus—a device designed to manipulate the fabric of reality itself.

"The separation must be complete," a younger Marcus Williams said, his voice echoing across time. "Magic is too powerful, too dangerous in its unified form. The only way to control it is to split it apart."

"The calculations are uncertain," another scientist protested. "Breaking such fundamental forces could have unforeseen consequences."

"The consequences of leaving magic whole are worse." Williams gestured to readouts showing magical energy patterns. "Already, we see people wielding power beyond our ability to contain. Better a controlled sundering than chaos."

The scientists moved through final preparations as reality itself held its breath. None of them understood what they were really about to do, that splitting magic would mean splitting everything—space, time, even souls.

The device was activated. Reality screamed.

And everything that was whole became divided.

The memory faded, leaving them gasping in the present. But it wasn't over. The nexus cycled again, showing them more.

Years later, Williams stood in this same chamber, watching as young students—including Samantha and Connor—worked on magical theory projects. His expression was calculating as he observed their natural affinity for working together.

"It's happening again," he told another teacher. "Despite the Sundering, despite everything we did to keep magic divided, some of them are remembering, finding their other halves."

"Should we separate them?"

"No." Williams smiled coldly. "Let them work together for now. Their research might prove useful. But watch them carefully. If they get too close to the truth..."

In a flicker of temporal distortion, they glimpsed Williams in his private quarters later that same night, reviewing their power readings with a different expression entirely—not clinical interest, but unmistakable fear tinged with envy.

"Two first-year students," he muttered to himself, "channeling more raw power than my entire family lineage combined." He pulled up records, displaying the Williams family tree alongside power metrics

spanning generations. *"Three centuries of carefully cultivated magical ability, three centuries of guiding civilization's development... potentially rendered irrelevant by children stumbling into unity."*

He closed the files with a gesture that betrayed contained fury. "The separation isn't just about safety. It's about the appropriate distribution of power. Some must lead; others must follow. That's the natural order—my family's order."

The vision shifted one final time.

It was the night Connor found the sealed records, the truth about what had been done. Williams confronted him in the archives.

"You don't understand what you've discovered," Williams said as shadow magic gathered around Connor, "what maintaining order requires."

"You didn't maintain order," Connor shot back. "You broke everything, split people apart who were meant to be whole."

"For the greater good. Magic was too powerful and too dangerous when unified. The Sundering saved civilization itself."

"It destroyed what we really were. And now you're trying to harness unified magic anyway, running experiments on your own people?"

Williams' expression hardened. "Some prices must be paid for progress. For control."

The fight that followed left Connor wounded but alive, running into exile while Williams began spinning the story of his betrayal.

The memories released them. Samantha found herself on her knees, Connor beside her, as their minds struggled to process what they'd seen, what they'd remembered.

"They did it on purpose," she whispered. "Split everything apart. Split us apart. Just for control."

"And now they're trying to master unified magic themselves," Connor added. "Even though forcing it is tearing reality apart."

Emma had moved to guard the chamber entrance, but her expression showed she'd seen enough. "So how do we stop them?"

Before they could answer, alarms blared throughout the Academy. Reality rippled as massive surges of magical energy pulsed through the facility.

"Williams," Connor snarled. "He's trying to stabilize the Convergence effects, force them into patterns he can control."

Samantha checked the readings on a nearby console. "He's making it worse. The temporal stability is—"

The chamber shuddered as another surge hit. Through the windows, they saw parts of the Academy stretching into impossible configurations while others collapsed in on themselves.

"We need to reach the main archives," Samantha decided. "Find the original Sundering research. Understand exactly what they did so we can undo it properly."

"Before Williams tears reality apart trying to control it," Connor agreed.

Emma's weapon hummed as she charged it. "Company coming. Reading multiple pursuit teams converging on our position."

They had minutes at most. But the path to the archives would take longer, even without reality distorting around them.

Unless...

"The nexus," Samantha said. "It's still connected to key points throughout the Academy, places important to the original Sundering."

Connor caught her meaning immediately. "Including the archives. We could use it to create a temporary pathway. But the power required..."

"We'd have to merge our magic completely," Samantha finished, "more deeply than we ever have before."

The implications hung between them. Merging magic at that level meant merging everything—thoughts, memories, the fragments of soul the Sundering had torn apart. They would remember exactly who they were before the split.

"Do it," Emma said from the doorway. "Whatever it takes. Just do it fast."

Reality twisted again as Williams' efforts further destabilized the Academy. They were out of options and out of time.

"Together?" Connor asked, holding out his hand.

Samantha took it without hesitation. "Together."

Their magic merged, light and shadow becoming something older, something whole. The nexus responded, temporal energies swirling as they forced open a pathway through broken space-time.

And as their power merged completely, they remembered everything.

Who they had been.

What had been stolen from them.

And exactly what it would take to make things right.

The truth waited in the archives, along with Williams and his forces.

Time to finish what the Sundering had started.

One way or another.

THIRTEEN
SHATTERED MIRRORS

The temporal pathway blazed with unified magic as Samantha and Connor stepped through, their merged consciousness struggling to process centuries of restored memories. They were still themselves, but also something more—something older that had been torn apart.

Their unity flowed like a remembered song, mathematical and true. Not Williams' forced combination of powers, but something older—something whole. Through their merged consciousness, they felt what they'd always known but never understood: they weren't combining magic; they were remembering it.

The contrast was written in reality itself. Where Williams' experiments left reality scarred and bleeding, their unified magic created patterns of perfect symmetry—fractals of light and shadow that reality recognized and embraced. They weren't forcing new configurations; they were revealing original truths.

Emma followed close behind, weapon ready. "Guards approaching from multiple vectors. Reality's getting more unstable by the minute."

Samantha nodded, trying to focus through the flood of memories. She remembered life before the Sundering when magic had been whole—remembered being whole. But those memories warred with her training, with everything the Federation had taught about the necessity of divided magic.

"The archives are three levels up," Connor said, his shadows now threaded with golden light. "Or they were before Williams started warping local space-time."

They moved through corridors that twisted impossibly, using their unified magic to stabilize reality around them. It was easier now, natural in a way that made the Federation's forced joining of powers seem crude and destructive.

Through their connection, they felt the fundamental difference. Williams and his followers tried to mathematically force Luminor and Tenebral magics to combine, like welding metals that were never meant to merge. But their unity wasn't a combination—it was recognition. Each pulse of their merged power showed them more: they weren't two separate beings learning to work together but one consciousness that had been artificially divided.

The Federation's teachings about separate magical forces crumbled against this deeper truth. In the spaces between moments, they glimpsed their original state—not Luminor and Tenebral, not even light and shadow, but something whole that had been broken apart for the sake of control.

"Multiple temporal signatures ahead," Emma reported, checking readings on her tactical display. "Looks like—"

Reality buckled. The corridor ahead split into three versions of itself, each leading to a different time period. Through the temporal distortion, they saw Academy security teams advancing, past, present, and possible future versions, all armed and ready.

"Well, that's new," Emma muttered.

Samantha assessed the situation with both tactical training and restored knowledge. "The temporal split is weakening local space-time. If we can—"

"Use it against them," Connor finished, their thoughts aligned through merged magic. "Create a recursive loop in the security teams' timeline."

They moved in perfect synchronization, unified power reaching out to twist the temporal energies. The security teams found themselves caught in a moment of endlessly repeating time, unable to advance or retreat.

"That won't hold them long," Samantha said. "Williams will notice the manipulation."

"He already has." Connor pointed ahead, where reality rippled with approaching power. "He's trying to stabilize the temporal field, force everything back into normal space-time."

They felt his efforts like hammer blows against reality itself. Williams wasn't even trying to be subtle anymore; he was just forcing his will on fundamental forces he didn't fully understand.

"The archives," Emma reminded them. "Before he tears the whole Academy apart."

They pressed on, navigating spaces that sometimes existed in multiple times simultaneously. Their merged memories helped them recognize patterns in the chaos and understand how reality wanted to flow when not forced into artificial separation.

But the restored memories brought other challenges.

"I remember the day they did it," Samantha said as they climbed a stairway that looped back on itself, "when they first split magic apart. We were there in our original form. We tried to stop them."

"They weren't ready for unified beings," Connor agreed. "Didn't understand what they were really destroying." His expression darkened. "But Williams understood. He knew exactly what the Sundering would do to us and did it anyway."

"And now he's trying to control unified magic himself." Samantha's laugh held no humor. "The irony would be amusing if it weren't destroying reality."

Another surge rocked the Academy. Through nearby windows, they saw entire sections of the facility twisting into impossible geometries as Williams fought to impose order on chaos.

"He's getting desperate," Connor observed. "The Convergence is accelerating faster than he expected. His containment measures are failing."

"Good," Emma said. "Maybe he'll tear himself apart before—"

"No." Samantha's voice was firm. "If he loses control completely, the feedback will destroy everything—not just the Academy, the whole sector."

They reached a junction where three corridors met at angles that shouldn't have been possible. Reality itself seemed thin here as if the space between moments might tear at any second.

"The archives are through there." Connor pointed to a doorway that flickered between locations. "But with these distortions..."

"We'll need to stabilize the local space-time field," Samantha finished, "create a bubble of normal reality long enough to reach the records."

Emma checked their rear approach. "How long will that take? Because we've got more company coming."

Samantha felt the approaching forces—Federation troops augmented with Williams' artificial unified magic. Their power signatures felt wrong, like badly tuned instruments forced to play together.

"Cover us," she told Emma. "This will take everything we've got."

As Emma took up a defensive position, Samantha and Connor faced the distorted space around the archive entrance. Their unified magic reached out, trying to impose order on chaos without forcing it.

The difference between their approach and Williams' was fundamental. Where he tried to control reality, to force it into patterns he understood, they worked with it, letting it flow naturally through their combined power.

Reality responded. The space around them began to stabilize, temporal distortions smoothing out as their magic restored proper order. For a moment, Samantha glimpsed what the Academy had once been—before the Sundering, before everything was broken apart.

Then Williams struck back.

His power slammed into their workings like a hammer, trying to force reality back into his preferred configuration. The battle of opposing magics sent temporal shock waves through the Academy.

"Incoming!" Emma opened fire as Federation troops appeared at both ends of the corridor. Their weapons crackled with artificial unified magic as they advanced.

Samantha felt Connor's thoughts align with hers as they split their focus. Part of their power maintained the space-time bubble while the rest defended against Williams' attacks. It should have been impossible to concentrate on both, but their merged consciousness handled it naturally.

This was how magic was meant to work, how they were meant to work.

"The entrance is stabilizing," Connor reported. "But Williams is—"

Another surge hit, stronger than before. Reality screamed as Williams poured more power into his attacks, trying to overwhelm their defenses through sheer force.

"He's going to tear everything apart." Samantha's jaw tightened. "He doesn't understand what he's doing."

Or maybe he did. Maybe he was desperate enough to risk everything rather than let them reach the archives, let them find proof of what he'd done.

"Commander!" Emma's warning came just as temporal distortions rippled through the Federation troops. Some vanished and shifted to other time periods. Others merged with alternate versions of themselves, their screams cutting off as reality rejected the paradox.

"Now!" Samantha called. "While the field is disrupted."

They pushed more power into their workings, stabilizing a path to the archive entrance. Reality fought them, torn between Williams' brutal forcing and their more natural approach.

"Go!" Connor thrust his shadows out, creating a barrier against approaching troops. "Get to the archives. Find the records."

"Not without you," Samantha started to protest.

"Together," he reminded her, taking her hand. Their unified magic surged stronger. "Always together now."

Emma laid down covering fire as they raced for the entrance. Behind them, reality began to collapse as Williams redoubled his efforts to stop them.

But they were already through, into the archives themselves, a space that existed somewhat outside normal time.

And there, waiting in the center of the room, stood Marcus Williams.

"I wondered when you'd remember," he said calmly, the artificial unified magic still crackling around him. Though his expression remained composed, micro-tremors in his hands and the slight unevenness of his breathing betrayed the strain of channeling forces never meant to be artificially merged.

For just a moment, as their unified magic flared in response to his presence, something flashed across his face—not just scientific concern, but a deeply personal fear. His eyes tracked the effortless harmony of their combined power with barely concealed apprehension.

"Shame you had to do it now, when my family is so close to controlling it properly. Generations of work, almost complete. Do you know what unified practitioners like you would do to the carefully balanced power structures we've maintained for centuries?"

"Close to destroying everything, you mean," Samantha corrected.

Williams smiled, and reality shuddered around them. "That depends entirely on your point of view—and how much you're willing to sacrifice for the greater good."

The battle for the Academy—for truth itself—was about to begin.

And reality held its breath to see who would win.

FOURTEEN
THE COST OF KNOWLEDGE

Williams' artificial unified magic crackled around him like broken glass, each surge sending ripples through local reality. The archive room stretched and compressed as temporal distortions intensified, centuries of magical knowledge threatening to tear itself apart.

"You know," Williams said conversationally, "I had such hopes for you two—my brightest students, naturally drawing together despite everything we did to keep unified souls separate."

"You mean everything you did to break reality itself?" Samantha's unified magic flowed in harmony with Connor's, golden light and shadow moving as one.

"Reality was already broken." Williams gestured, sending a wave of forced power toward them. "Magic was too strong, too dangerous in its original form. The Sundering saved civilization."

They deflected his attack together, their merged consciousness processing battle tactics instantly. But the archive room's compressed space made proper maneuvering impossible.

"Saved it?" Connor's shadows probed the distorted air, seeking weaknesses. "You destroyed what we really are, split everyone apart just so you could control them."

"Control was necessary... is necessary. Look around you. Even now, the Convergence threatens to tear everything apart. Without proper control—"

"The only thing tearing reality apart is you." Samantha saw the patterns in his artificial magic, the forced merging of powers that should flow together naturally. "Your experiments, your attempts to control unified magic, they're accelerating the collapse."

Emma moved quietly along the archive's edge, weapon ready. But Williams noticed her positioning.

"Ah yes, the loyal soldier." His smile was cold. "Still following orders even after learning the truth. That's what the Federation does best, isn't it? Creates good followers."

"You're insane," Emma said flatly. "What you did to magic, to people—"

"Was necessary!" Reality shuddered as Williams' control slipped. Blood vessels darkened beneath his skin as the power coursed through him, but his eyes showed not madness but fierce conviction. "You think small, think only of individuals. But I saw the larger picture, saw what unified magic could do if left unchecked. I've run the models thousands of times—the math doesn't lie. Without proper controls, without separation, catastrophic misuse isn't just possible—it's inevitable. My family has dedicated generations to preventing that future."

While he spoke, Samantha and Connor stretched their senses through the archives. Somewhere in this temporal maze waited records of the original Sundering, evidence of what Williams had done.

He noticed their attention shift. "Looking for proof? Don't bother. Those records are long gone. Destroyed when we—"

"When did you realize some people were remembering?" Connor pressed. "When did your perfect separation start to break down?"

Williams' expression darkened. "Anomalies. Errors in the process. But we learned from those mistakes. The new process will be perfect."

The implications hit them all at once. Samantha felt Connor's horror merge with her own as understanding dawned.

"You're planning another Sundering," she breathed. "Using the Convergence itself to—"

"To remake reality properly this time." Williams raised his hands, and the archive room twisted impossibly. "No more anomalies. No more souls finding their other halves. Pure, perfect separation."

They struck before he finished speaking, unified magic lashing out in precisely coordinated patterns. For a moment, Williams' defenses buckled under their combined assault.

But he'd been preparing for this moment for too long.

Reality screamed as he forced more power through his artificial connections. The archive room fractured into multiple time streams, each version of the space overlapping chaotically.

"You see?" Williams called as they dodged temporal fragments. "This is what unified magic brings. Chaos. Destruction. The Sundering was necessary then, and it's necessary now."

"The only chaos here is yours," Connor shot back. Their unified magic created a bubble of stable space around them, letting them move through the temporal distortions.

Williams smiled. "Are you sure about that?"

He gestured again, but this time, his attack wasn't aimed at them.

Emma had been moving into position for a clear shot, using their confrontation as cover. But Williams had seen her and planned for it.

Reality twisted.

Emma fired.

Time shattered.

Everything happened at once: Emma's shot passing through spaces that shouldn't exist, Williams' counter-attack bending temporal laws, their unified magic trying to stabilize local reality.

When space-time reasserted itself, Emma lay crumpled against the archive walls, blood seeping from wounds that existed in multiple moments simultaneously.

"Emma!" Samantha started toward her, but Williams' power cut her off.

"An object lesson," he said calmly, "in the dangers of unified magic, in why the Sundering was necessary—is necessary."

Connor's shadows probed Emma's injuries while Samantha held Williams back. The wounds were bad—reality itself had torn through her.

"She needs medical attention," Connor reported, his voice tight. "These temporal injuries—"

"Will only get worse." Williams spread his hands. "As reality continues to break down. Unless..."

"Unless we let you perform another Sundering," Samantha finished, "to create your perfect separation."

"Now you understand." He smiled again, and reality rippled around them. "The choice is yours. Stay and watch your friend die as time itself bleeds through her wounds. Or..."

For a moment, his scientific facade cracked, revealing raw fear beneath the controlled exterior. "You don't understand what I've seen. The simulations don't just predict destruction—they show extinction! I stood in the ruins of Rosewood, measuring radiation from magic that had broken free of all constraint. Five hundred square miles rendered uninhabitable. Over a million dead from one person's loss of control."

His eyes fixed on their combined power with a mixture of scientific fascination and profound dread. "Look at you—two individuals channeling more power than my entire research division. Do you understand what would happen if everyone could do that? If unified magic became common again? The mathematics are irrefutable."

He left the threat hanging. But they all felt reality growing more unstable by the second. Emma's breathing was shallow, her injuries defying normal space-time.

They needed to retreat, to regroup and find another way to stop Williams before he destroyed everything in his quest for control.

Samantha met Connor's eyes through their merged consciousness and felt his agreement with her tactical assessment.

"This isn't over," she told Williams.

"It never is." He watched calmly as they gathered Emma's injured form. "But next time we meet, reality itself will be at stake. Choose wisely."

They escaped through twisting corridors, using unified magic to stabilize space enough for movement. Behind them, Williams' laughter echoed through broken time streams.

Emma's wounds left traces of temporal energy in their wake—reality bleeding through the cracks Williams had created. They needed to get her help before the temporal damage became permanent.

But they'd seen enough in the archives. Glimpsed records Williams hadn't managed to destroy completely.

He wasn't just planning another Sundering.

He was planning to use the Convergence itself—reality's attempt to heal—as a weapon to break everything apart permanently.

And they were running out of time to stop him.

In more ways than one.

FIFTEEN
TEMPORAL WOUNDS

Time fractured around Emma's wounds, each injury existing in multiple states simultaneously. Blood appeared before cuts opened and healed before wounds formed—regular medical treatment would be useless against damage that ignored causality itself. They needed to stabilize her in normal space-time and do it quickly.

Samantha's jaw clenched as she poured more power into the containment field. "Emma, stay with us. Focus on my voice."

Emma's eyes flickered open, but her gaze wasn't focused on any single moment. "Commander? I see... everything's breaking apart. The Sundering is happening again. Going to happen. Already happened."

"That's the temporal displacement talking." Samantha traced mathematical patterns in the air, trying to isolate Emma in normal space-time. "Connor, the stabilization matrices?"

He nodded, shadows weaving complex geometries. Together, their unified magic created a bubble of stable reality around Emma's form. Inside that space, time would flow normally—at least temporarily.

"The wounds are settling into normal causality," Connor reported. "But without proper medical equipment—"

"We work with what we have." Samantha began treating the now-stabilized injuries, using unified magic to accelerate natural healing. "Emma, status?"

"Still seeing... echoes." Emma's voice was stronger but strained. "The archives. Williams... he's going to break everything again."

"Not if we stop him." Samantha checked the temporal readings around the wounds. "The bleeding's slowing, but you'll need to stay in the containment field until we can get proper treatment."

"No time," Emma protested. "The records we found—"

"Are safe." Connor held up a data crystal he'd managed to grab during their retreat. "Partial archives, but enough to prove what Williams did, and what he's planning."

While Emma rested, they began analyzing the recovered data. The crystal contained fragments of the original Sundering research, including technical specifications that made Samantha's blood run cold.

"They didn't just separate magic," she said, studying the documents. "They created a recursive temporal loop, ensuring the separation would propagate backward and forward through time. Making it seem like magic had always been divided."

"Rewriting history itself," Connor agreed. "But they couldn't completely eliminate what came before. That's why some people still remember, still find their other halves despite the separation."

Emma shifted in her containment field. "Like you two?"

They exchanged glances through their merged consciousness. The connection between them felt more natural with each passing moment, as if their souls were remembering their original state.

"The Convergence is reality trying to heal itself," Samantha said, "trying to restore what was broken. But Williams plans to use that same energy to create an even stronger separation."

"One that can't be overcome," Connor added. "No more unified souls finding each other. No more remembering what was lost. Perfect, permanent control."

"And if he fails?" Emma asked.

"Then reality tears itself apart completely." Samantha's voice was grim. "The Convergence is too strong now, too close to completion. Trying to force another Sundering through it would be like detonating a bomb inside a fusion reactor."

They studied the technical data, looking for weaknesses in Williams' plan. But the more they understood, the worse things appeared.

"He's modified the original Sundering device," Connor said, highlighting specific sections, "using Academy students as test subjects to refine the process. That's what happened in those 'training accidents' we heard about."

"And now he's ready to implement the final version"—Samantha traced the energy patterns in the designs—"using the Convergence itself as a power source. The temporal backlash alone would—"

She broke off as reality shuddered around them. Even through the maintenance sector's shielding, they felt Williams continued experiments distorting space-time.

"We're running out of time," Emma said quietly. "Commander... what's our play here?"

Samantha studied the technical readouts while Connor probed the local reality distortions with his shadows. They needed a plan to stop Williams without destroying everything.

"The original Sundering device," Samantha said finally. "It's still in the Academy somewhere. Has to be, for his plan to work."

Connor caught her meaning immediately. "If we can reach it first, understand exactly how it works..."

"We might be able to reverse the process." Samantha's mind raced through possibilities. "Not just stop Williams, but undo what was done. Heal reality properly instead of letting it tear itself apart."

"The cost would be enormous," Connor warned. "That much unified magic, trying to rewrite centuries of artificial separation..."

"Better than Williams' plan." Emma tried to sit up, then fell back as temporal distortions rippled through her wounds. "But I won't be much help like this."

"You've done enough." Samantha checked the containment field again. "Rest. Let the temporal injuries stabilize. We'll need you ready when everything goes down."

They spent the next hour planning, studying the partial archives for any advantage they could find. The original Sundering device would be heavily guarded, probably deep in the Academy's most secure sections. And Williams would be expecting them to try something.

But they had one advantage he couldn't counter: truly unified magic, working the way it was meant to work. His artificial joining of powers might be strong, but it wasn't natural. It wasn't whole.

"We'll need a distraction," Connor said, outlining tactical approaches. "Something to keep Williams occupied while we locate the device."

"And a way to shield ourselves from temporal backlash once we start the reversal process." Samantha gestured to Emma's injuries. "One mistake with cause and effect at that level..."

"About that." Emma's voice was quiet but firm. "The temporal bleeding... I'm seeing things. Things that haven't happened yet. Will happen. Must happen."

They turned to her, concerned by her tone.

"What kind of things?" Samantha asked.

Emma met their eyes steadily. "The cost. What fixing reality will really require." She swallowed hard. "You're not going to like it."

The maintenance sector's shielding hummed as another reality distortion rippled through the Academy. Time was running out.

One way or another, everything was about to change.

The only question was, what price would change demand?

And who would have to pay it?

SIXTEEN

THE HEART OF BREAKING

The Academy's lower levels weren't just shielded from reality distortions—they were shielded from reality itself. As Samantha and Connor descended deeper into the facility's original construction, their unified magic revealed layers of temporal manipulation stretching back centuries.

"The whole foundation is built on broken time," Connor observed, his shadows probing the walls. "They didn't just split magic here. They anchored the Sundering into the physical structure."

Emma followed in her containment field, moving slowly but steadily. The temporal bleeding had stabilized enough for careful movement, though echo images of her injuries still flickered in and out of existence.

"These readings are impossible," she said, checking her sensors. "The temporal distortion levels... it's like this place exists partially outside normal space-time."

"That was the point." Samantha traced glowing patterns in the air, analyzing the facility's construction. "They needed somewhere reality's normal laws wouldn't apply, somewhere they could break everything without breaking themselves."

The deeper they went, the more their merged consciousness provided context for what they were seeing. The Academy's builders hadn't just created a school—they'd created a temple to artificial separation. Every stone had been laid with the purpose of maintaining the Sundering's effects.

They reached a massive door marked with symbols that hurt to look at directly—mathematical formulae that denied their own solutions, geometric patterns that violated basic physics.

"The original chamber," Connor said quietly. "Where they first split magic apart."

Samantha nodded, feeling reality twist around them. "And where Williams plans to do it again. But bigger this time. Permanent."

The door's locking mechanism was complex—a combination of technological security and mathematical wards designed to prevent unified magic from operating properly. But they weren't trying to unify separate magics. Their power was already whole, working the way it was meant to work.

The locks didn't stand a chance.

Inside, the chamber stretched impossibly in all directions. Reality bent around a central device that pulsed with wrongness—the original Sundering machine, modified and enhanced by Williams' modern additions.

"This is..." Emma's voice failed as she took in the scope of it. "The power readings are off the charts."

"Because it's not just drawing power from our time." Connor pointed to crystal structures surrounding the device. "He's built temporal collectors that are drawing energy from past and future simultaneously."

"He's using the Convergence itself as a power source." Samantha studied the machine's modifications. "The natural healing process becomes the weapon that breaks everything permanently."

They moved carefully through the chamber, analyzing Williams' preparations. The technical skill was impressive, even if its purpose was monstrous. He'd taken the original Sundering device and enhanced it with centuries of advanced theory.

"Look at these containment matrices," Connor said, gesturing to complex energy patterns. "He's not just planning to separate magic this time. He's going to..."

"Rewrite the fundamental laws of reality." Samantha finished. "Change how magic itself works, going back to the beginning of time. Make separation the natural state."

"Can he do that?" Emma asked, her containment field flickering as the chamber's temporal energies interfered with it.

"He's already doing it." Samantha pointed to readings showing reality distortions spreading throughout the sector. "Every experiment, every test... he's been laying the groundwork for years. The Convergence just gives him the power to complete it."

They found Williams' research stations and displays showing the progress of his work. The technical details confirmed their worst fears. He wasn't just planning another Sundering—he was planning to make it retroactive through all of time.

"These power calculations..." Connor highlighted specific sections. "The temporal feedback alone would—"

"Tear reality apart at the seams." Samantha's voice was grim.

"He's so focused on control, he doesn't see what he's really doing. Or doesn't care."

Emergency alerts flashed across the displays. Throughout the Academy, reality distortions were reaching critical levels. Williams' experiments had weakened the barriers between moments too much.

"Time's breaking down faster than he predicted," Connor reported, analyzing the data. "The Convergence is accelerating, trying to heal the damage. But his attempts to control it are making everything worse."

"How long?" Emma asked.

Samantha checked the readings. "Hours at most. Once the cascade begins..." She let the thought hang. They all knew what would happen.

"So we stop him." Emma's voice was steady despite her injuries. "Use this device ourselves. Reverse what they did."

"It's not that simple." Connor's shadows traced the machine's structure. "The original Sundering was powered by unified magic torn forcibly apart. Reversing it would require..."

"The willing sacrifice of unified magic," Samantha finished, "given freely to heal rather than break."

The implications settled over them. They had unified magic now, working naturally together—the power to potentially undo what had been done.

But the cost...

"Commander." Emma's voice cut through their thoughts. "The temporal bleeding... I'm seeing possibilities. Futures. In most of them, everything ends here. Reality tears itself apart as Williams tries to force his plan through."

"And in the others?"

Emma met their eyes steadily. "You know what has to happen, what the price would be."

Before they could respond, reality shuddered around them. The chamber's temporal shielding flickered as waves of distortion rippled through the Academy.

"He's starting," Connor said, checking readings, "channeling power from the Convergence into the device."

"Without understanding what he's really doing." Samantha moved to the central controls. "The Convergence isn't just reality trying to heal itself. It's everything that was broken trying to be whole again. Magic, space, time..."

"Souls," Connor added quietly.

They felt Williams' power building throughout the Academy. He was drawing energy from the Convergence itself, trying to turn reality's healing process into a weapon.

"We need to make a decision." Emma's voice was urgent. "Before he tears everything apart trying to control it."

Samantha and Connor exchanged glances through their merged consciousness. They'd seen the technical specs and understood what reversing the Sundering would require and the price it would demand.

"Together?" Connor asked.

"Always," Samantha replied.

Reality screamed around them as Williams began his final experiment.

Time to choose:

Let him break everything, trying to maintain control.

Or break themselves trying to make it whole again.

Their decision would change everything.

Forever.

SEVENTEEN
CRITICAL MASS

Reality fractured around them as they fought their way through the Academy's twisting corridors. Williams' attempt to channel the Convergence had triggered a cascade of temporal failures. Entire sections of the facility existed in multiple times simultaneously, while others had ceased existing altogether.

"The main power conduits are overloading," Emma reported from her containment field, checking readings on her tablet. "He's drawing too much energy too fast."

"Because he knows we're coming." Samantha's unified magic merged seamlessly with Connor's as they stabilized another corridor. "He's rushing the process, trying to complete it before we can stop him."

They rounded a corner and found themselves facing a squad of Federation troops. The soldiers moved wrongly, their bodies twisted by artificial unified magic as Williams forced them to channel power they were never meant to handle.

"These men are dying," Connor said quietly, his shadows

probing their corrupted life signs. "The forced unification is burning them out from the inside."

The troops attacked without speaking, their movements jerky and unnatural. Samantha and Connor's unified magic flowed together in precise patterns, containing rather than killing. These weren't enemies—they were victims.

"How many?" Samantha asked as they secured the unconscious soldiers. "How many people has he sacrificed for this?"

"Too many." Emma checked the troops' life signs. "And he's not done yet. These energy readings... he's going to need more channels. More people to burn through."

Another reality quake shook the Academy. Through nearby windows, they saw the sky itself beginning to tear. The Convergence's natural healing energy, twisted by Williams' efforts to control it, was starting to break down the basic fabric of space-time.

They fought their way through more security checkpoints, past more corrupted troops. Each confrontation showed them the cost of Williams' artificial unification—the price of trying to force power that should flow naturally.

"The central chamber's ahead," Connor reported, consulting architectural plans they'd recovered. "But these readings..." He broke off, shadows flickering with concern.

Samantha saw it too. The power levels were far beyond what they'd calculated. Williams wasn't just channeling the Convergence—he was trying to absorb its power directly.

"He's going to kill himself," she realized, "to try to become a conduit for the entire process."

"And take reality with him if he fails," Emma added. Her containment field flickered as another temporal wave passed through. "Which he will. The human body wasn't meant to channel that much power."

They reached a security station overlooking the central chamber. Through reinforced windows, they saw Williams standing at the heart of a massive energy matrix. Power from the Convergence itself flowed through him, turning his body into a grotesque puppet as he tried to control forces beyond mortal comprehension.

"The device..." Connor pointed to the modified Sundering machine. "He's connected it directly to his nervous system, using himself as a focusing mechanism."

"Because he knows artificial unification isn't enough." Samantha studied the energy patterns. "He needs a living conductor to handle this much power. To control the separation process directly."

Reality buckled again. Through the reinforced windows, they watched in horror as sections of the Academy began to fold in on themselves, crushed by Williams' attempts to rewrite fundamental laws.

"We need to shut it down." Emma's voice was urgent. "Before he—"

The security station's inner wall exploded inward.

Williams' power lashed out like a living thing, seeking them through the broken reality. They barely managed to shield themselves as temporal energy tore through the station.

"Did you think I wouldn't sense you coming?" Williams' voice echoed strangely, distorted by the power flowing through him. "I felt your unified magic the moment you entered the Academy. So pure, so natural..." His laugh held no humor. "So dangerous."

They scrambled for cover as another blast reduced the station to twisted metal. Through the debris, they saw Williams floating above the chamber floor, reality breaking and reforming around him with each breath.

"Look at him," Connor said quietly. "The power's already burning him out. He can't maintain that level of channeling for long."

"Long enough." Samantha weighed options as Williams continued to rant. "We need to separate him from the device. Break the connection before—"

"Before what?" Williams called. "Before I complete what we started centuries ago? Before I make the separation permanent?" Energy crackled around him. "You don't understand. You can't. Your unified magic blinds you to the necessity of control."

He gestured, and reality itself answered. The chamber's floor became a maze of temporal tears, each one leading to a different moment in time. The walls pulsed with power drawn from past and future simultaneously.

"The Convergence is too dangerous to allow," Williams continued. "Reality trying to heal itself? Restore what was broken? The fools who created unified magic never understood the need for limits. For control."

"The only thing out of control here is you," Samantha shot back. She felt Connor moving through the shadows, trying to find an angle on the device's power supply.

"Am I?" Williams smiled, and blood trickled from his eyes. "I've spent centuries preparing for this moment, planning how to use the Convergence itself to make the separation permanent— perfect."

He raised his hands, and reality screamed.

The chamber's temporal tears widened, showing glimpses of other times. They saw the original Sundering and reality being torn apart by Williams and his allies, saw the moment magic itself was split into opposing forces.

"Do you see the damage unified magic could cause?" Williams gestured to the scenes of devastation. "The chaos it brought? We saved civilization by breaking it apart. And now..."

His power pulsed stronger, drawing more energy from the Convergence. The device hummed as it channeled impossible amounts of power through his twisted form.

"Now we make it permanent," he finished. "No more unified souls finding each other. No more remembered connections. Pure, perfect separation. Forever."

They had seconds to act. Connor was almost in position, his shadows ready to sever the device's power conduits. Samantha prepared to launch a frontal assault, drawing Williams' attention.

But Emma saw it first.

"Commander!" Her warning came just as reality itself began to fold inward. The chamber's temporal tears were combining, creating a singularity of broken time centered on Williams himself.

They barely managed to shield themselves as the temporal wave hit. When they could see again, the chamber had changed. Reality itself was beginning to unravel around Williams as he drew more power from the Convergence.

"It's starting," he said, his voice distorted by the energy flowing through him. "The final separation. The end of unified magic. The end of everything it threatens."

They had one chance left. One opportunity to stop him before reality itself broke under the strain.

But the cost...

The cost would be higher than any of them had imagined.

And they were out of time to find another way.

140

EIGHTEEN
THE PRICE OF UNITY

The chamber had become a maelstrom of temporal energy as Williams channeled more power from the Convergence. Reality itself bent around him, trying to accommodate forces it was never meant to contain. Through the chaos, Samantha and Connor saw the truth of what the original Sundering had been—and what reversing it would cost.

"The calculations were wrong," Connor said, his shadows probing the energy patterns around Williams. "They didn't just split magic apart. They split everything. Reality, time, souls... all of it divided to maintain control."

"And now he's trying to make it permanent," Samantha's unified magic merged with Connor's, creating a bubble of stable space around them and Emma, "using the Convergence itself as a weapon against unity."

Williams floated above them, power crackling through his twisted form. Blood flowed freely from his eyes and ears as his body struggled to contain the energy he was channeling.

"You still don't understand," he called, his voice distorted by power. "The Convergence isn't reality trying to heal—it's chaos trying to destroy everything we built, everything my family sacrificed to maintain order."

As their unified magic rose to meet his artificial power, Williams' expression betrayed a moment of raw personal terror. "Look at you—natural unity gives you power my family has spent generations trying to achieve through science and control. Do you think civilization can survive when anyone could potentially wield such force? When the carefully maintained hierarchies that govern our society collapse?"

Blood flowed freely from his eyes as his body struggled to contain the channels of power. "I was like you once. I believed unified magic could be controlled safely. The Rosewood aftermath changed everything. Standing in that devastation, seeing what one person's loss of control could do..." His voice faltered, the mask of scientific concern briefly slipping to reveal the fear beneath: fear of irrelevance, fear of losing his family's position.

He gestured to the temporal tears, where glimpses of catastrophic destruction flickered. "One practitioner," Williams said, voice tight with remembered horror, "one unified mage lost control and destroyed everything within five hundred miles. Imagine thousands with that power, imagine what happens when they inevitably fight. This burden falls to those who understand the cost of failure—who are willing to make the hard choices that preserve civilization itself."

The modified Sundering device pulsed with impossible energy as Williams drew more power through it. Around them, reality continued to fragment. Through temporal tears in the chamber walls, they saw other times, other possibilities—including what the world had been before the original Sundering.

"Look." Williams gestured to the tears in space-time. "Look at what unified magic brought. Chaos. Destruction. Power beyond control. We had to break it apart. Had to impose order."

"You imposed artificial separation," Samantha countered, "broke apart things that were meant to be whole."

"Because whole was dangerous. Unified magic, unified souls—too much power in too few hands." Williams laughed, the sound distorted by the energy flowing through him. "Better to break everything apart than risk losing control."

Emma's containment field flickered as another temporal wave passed through the chamber. Despite her injuries, she was already analyzing patterns, identifying weak points in the Academy's structure—not just physical, but institutional. If they survived this, everything would need to be rebuilt. And somehow, she knew that task would fall to her.

"Commander, these readings... reality itself is starting to break down. The artificial separation is becoming unstable."

"Because it was never meant to be permanent," Connor said. His shadows traced complex patterns in the air, analyzing the energy flows. "The cosmos wants to be whole. The Convergence is just the natural order trying to restore itself."

"Natural order brings chaos!" Williams' power surged stronger, drawing more energy from the Convergence. "But I've found a way to make the separation permanent, to rewrite the fundamental laws of existence itself."

The device hummed louder as Williams pushed more power through it. Through the temporal tears, they saw the moment of the original Sundering—saw existence itself being torn apart by Williams and his allies.

But they also saw something else.

"There." Samantha pointed to a specific energy pattern in the device. "The original calculations didn't account for unified consciousness, for souls finding their other halves despite the separation."

Connor saw it too. "Because they couldn't. Natural unity is stronger than artificial separation. That's why some people still remember and still find each other despite everything they did to keep us apart."

"And that's why it has to end." Williams raised his hands, and the fabric of existence screamed around them. "No more unified souls. No more remembered connections. Pure, perfect separation for all time."

But they'd seen enough. Through their merged consciousness, Samantha and Connor understood exactly what reversing the Sundering would require, what price would have to be paid to restore what was broken.

"Emma," Samantha called. "The temporal readings from your injuries... what did you see? What future possibilities?"

Emma's expression was grim. "You know what I saw, what has to happen. The price..."

"Has to be paid willingly," Connor finished. "Unified magic given freely to heal rather than forced apart to control."

Williams must have sensed their understanding. His power lashed out, trying to disrupt their connection, but their unified magic held strong, working the way it was meant to.

His artificial unified magic crackled with wrongness, each pulse leaving traces of corruption in space-time. But where his power tried to force the cosmos to obey, their natural unity sang with mathematical perfection. The difference wasn't just in strength or technique—it was fundamental, like the difference between forcing a lock and turning a key that fits perfectly.

Through their merged consciousness, they felt other pairs throughout the Academy responding to their presence. Dormant connections awoke, and artificial barriers fell away as existence remembered its true nature. Williams could force magic to combine, but he couldn't replicate what they had—the resonance of souls remembering they were meant to be one.

"You can't stop this," he snarled. "The separation is necessary. Control is necessary. Without it—"

"Without it, existence heals itself," Samantha cut him off. "Magic becomes whole again. Everything becomes whole again."

"And the price?" Williams smiled through his bleeding eyes. "Are you prepared to pay it, to give up everything you are to restore what was broken?"

They were. Through their merged consciousness, they felt the truth of what needed to be done. Unified magic could heal what was broken—but only if given freely, only if those with the power to restore unity were willing to sacrifice themselves in the process.

The cosmos shuddered around them as Williams drew even more power from the Convergence. The device's hum had become a scream as it channeled impossible amounts of energy through his dying body.

"It's time to choose," he called. "Let me complete the separation. Make it permanent. Or watch existence tear itself apart as the Convergence tries to restore what should stay broken."

But there was a third choice.

Samantha felt Connor's agreement through their merged consciousness. Their unified magic hummed between them, ready to be given—ready to heal rather than break.

"Together?" he asked quietly.

"Always," she replied.

They had found each other despite centuries of artificial separation, remembered who they were despite everything done to keep them apart.

Now, it was time to use that unity to restore what was broken.

Even if it meant breaking themselves in the process.

The choice was made.

The price would be paid.

And existence itself held its breath to see what would come next.

NINETEEN
THE FINAL UNITY

The fabric of existence bent and twisted as Samantha and Connor stepped forward, their unified magic blazing against Williams' artificial power. The chamber had become a nexus of temporal energy, past and present colliding as the Convergence fought against forced separation.

"You can't stop this," Williams snarled, blood streaming from his eyes as he channeled more power through the device. "The separation must be maintained, must be made permanent!"

"No." Their voices merged as their unified magic reached out. "It's time to heal what was broken."

The battle that followed existed in multiple times simultaneously. Through the temporal distortions, they glimpsed other Academy staff and students making choices—some clinging to the old order, others reaching instinctively toward unity. The head instructor of theoretical magic placed herself between Federation troops and her students. A young cadet helped his former enemies find shelter from the cosmic breakdown. Small moments of choice would shape what was to come.

Williams hurled fragments of broken existence at them, trying to tear them apart. But their unified magic moved naturally, flowing the way it was meant to flow, deflecting his desperate attacks.

"You'll destroy everything!" Williams' power crackled wildly as his body began to fail. "Without control, without separation—"

"The cosmos heals itself," they answered together. Their unified magic pressed forward, golden light and shadow working as one to contain his artificial power.

Emma watched from her containment field, monitoring the stress levels in the fabric of existence. "The temporal fractures are reaching critical mass. Whatever you're going to do..."

They understood. Williams' desperate channeling of the Convergence had pushed the cosmos to its breaking point. They had moments to act before everything shattered completely.

Together, they reached out to the modified Sundering device. Their unified magic touched its core, feeling the mathematical patterns that had broken reality apart centuries ago, the equations that had split everything—magic, time, souls—into artificially separated pieces.

"Don't!" Williams tried to stop them, but his power was failing. His body couldn't contain the energy he'd forced through it. "You'll undo everything we built, everything we sacrificed to maintain order!"

"Order through broken existence isn't order at all." Their unified magic began to rewrite the device's core patterns. "It's time to restore what was meant to be whole."

Williams screamed as they severed his connection to the device. His artificial unification collapsed, leaving him sprawled on the chamber floor, bloody and broken but alive.

But stopping him was only the beginning.

The device's temporal matrices still hummed with power drawn from the Convergence. Existence itself waited to be either permanently broken or finally healed.

"The calculations are ready," they said, their merged consciousness processing centuries of magical theory in moments. "Emma, get clear. What comes next..."

"I know." Her voice was steady despite her injuries. "The temporal bleeding showed me everything."

They began the final sequence, their unified magic flowing into the device. But instead of using it to force existence apart, they offered their power freely, offered themselves to heal what had been broken.

The chamber shuddered as the cosmic fabric recognized their intent. The temporal tears began to shift, showing not just what had been but what could be—what should have been, had the artificial separation not been forced on everything.

"It's responding," Emma reported, checking readings. "The Convergence... it's changing pattern. Instead of fighting against control..."

"It's accepting freely given unity," they finished. The device hummed as they poured more power into it, their merged consciousness directing the healing process.

Through the temporal tears, they saw the original Sundering playing out, saw Williams and his allies forcing existence apart, breaking everything to impose their version of control. But now they saw how to reverse it. How to heal rather than break.

The cost would be enormous. They could feel it already as existence began to reshape itself around their offering. Their unified magic, their merged consciousness, their very beings would be consumed in the process of restoration.

But it was their choice, their willing sacrifice to heal what should never have been broken.

"Commander!" Emma called urgently. "The temporal field is collapsing. Existence is trying to rewrite itself, but the stress levels..."

They understood. The change had to be guided carefully, or existence would tear itself apart in the process of healing. They had to direct the restoration and shape it with their unified magic until the very end.

"It's starting," they said together, their voices merging as existence began to shift around them. The device pulsed with power as they fed their unified magic into it, freely giving everything they were to heal everything that had been broken.

Williams stirred on the chamber floor, his eyes widening as he saw what was happening. "No... you'll destroy everything..."

"We'll restore everything," they corrected. Their unified magic blazed brighter as existence continued to reform around them. "Not through force, not through control, but through willing sacrifice."

The chamber filled with light as the process reached its peak. Through the temporal tears, they saw existence beginning to heal, artificial separation giving way to natural unity, and everything that had been broken starting to become whole.

Emma's containment field flickered as her temporal injuries began to stabilize. Existence itself was healing, restoring proper time flow and proper unity.

But the cost...

They felt it as their unified magic poured into the device, felt themselves beginning to fade as existence reshaped itself. Their merged consciousness was becoming part of the restoration, their willing sacrifice powering the healing of everything that had been broken.

"Commander," Emma's voice reached them through the light. "Samantha, Connor... thank you."

They smiled as existence continued to change around them. This was right. This was necessary. This was how magic was meant to work—given freely to heal rather than forced apart to control.

But even as they felt themselves dissolving into the greater pattern, as their individual selves became part of something larger, they weren't afraid.

They were together.

They were whole.

And through their sacrifice, everything else would be whole again too.

The mathematics of their unity had always been beautiful, but now it became something more—a living equation that rewrote the fundamental laws of existence, replacing artificial separation with natural harmony.

Their love had transcended institutional lies, conquered artificial barriers, and now it would heal the deepest wound ever inflicted on reality itself.

The price of unity was everything they were.

But unity itself was worth any price.

As the light grew brighter around them, as their consciousness merged completely with the healing process, they felt the cosmos itself respond to their gift. Reality was remembering its original state, and artificial barriers were dissolving like dreams at dawn.

Their last coherent thought was wonder at the beauty of it—how existence sang when it was finally allowed to be whole.

TWENTY
PRIVATE RECKONING

Marcus Williams sat alone in his private study, watching displays that showed the Academy's reality stabilizing around him. His body ached from the artificial unification experiments, burned by channeling power it was never meant to contain. Around him, the Williams family legacy pressed down like a weight he could no longer bear.

Through his window, he could see the memorial garden where Reed and Blake's sacrifice had created something he'd spent his life trying to prevent—a stable nexus of natural unified magic. Their power hadn't destroyed anything.

It had healed.

The realization cut through decades of carefully constructed certainties. He called up the data from their final working, studying energy patterns that defied everything his models predicted. Where artificial unification left reality scarred and bleeding, their natural unity had created mathematical perfection.

They weren't forcing new laws onto existence. They were revealing what had always been there.

Marcus pulled up Sarah's final message from Rosewood, her voice somehow preserved in the facility's emergency recordings.

"Stop this. Whatever it takes. Don't let this happen to anyone else."

For fifty years, he'd interpreted those words as a mandate to prevent unified magic from manifesting. But watching the memorial garden pulse with healing energy, he understood her true meaning. She hadn't been asking him to prevent unified magic—she'd been asking him to prevent the institutional constraints that had made her tragedy inevitable.

The Academy's reality distortions were stabilizing as he released his experimental controls. Each system he powered down felt like shedding a weight he'd carried too long. The Convergence's energy flowed naturally now, seeking harmony rather than fighting his forced patterns.

No explosions. No reality storms. No loss of control.

Just magic working as it should.

Marcus thought of his family's legacy, of the institutional frameworks built on his theories about unified magic's dangers. Four generations of Williams had dedicated their lives to preventing what he now saw might be natural healing.

But how could he explain this reversal? How could he tell them that everything they'd worked for might be wrong?

His personal files remained sealed, his private research locked away from even his closest family members. The Williams organization expected clear guidance, unambiguous direction. To admit uncertainty now would undermine everything they'd built.

He stood and walked to his window, looking out at Academy grounds that no longer writhed with temporal distortions. The

Convergence was completing its work, healing what had been artificially broken.

His experimental systems powered down one by one, their artificial unity dissolving as he released his hold on forces he'd never truly controlled. Each shutdown felt like another step toward honesty, toward accepting what the evidence clearly showed.

The memorial fountain in the garden caught his attention. Water danced with increasing complexity, patterns that spoke of harmony rather than destruction. Even from this distance, he could sense the mathematical elegance of its flow.

This was what unified magic looked like when approached with wisdom instead of fear.

Marcus activated the Academy's communication system. Throughout the facility, his voice would carry to every classroom, every laboratory, every corner where the next generation of magical practitioners trained.

"This is Dr. Marcus Williams," he began, his words reaching students and teachers alike. "I am releasing all experimental controls on Convergence energy. What follows is reality's natural healing process. Do not attempt to contain or redirect it. Simply... let it flow."

The response was immediate. Through his displays, he watched as reality settled into patterns of unprecedented stability. The Academy's temporal distortions faded completely, replaced by the gentle rhythm of natural unified magic.

Sarah would have loved this, he realized. The beauty of it, the mathematical elegance, the way existence itself seemed to breathe more easily as artificial constraints dissolved.

But what would his family make of his decision? They would see it as defeat, as abandonment of everything the Williams name represented. They would demand explanations he couldn't give, certainties he no longer possessed.

Marcus sealed his personal research files with the highest security classifications. His doubts, his growing questions about the family's mission—these would remain private. The Williams organization needed clear leadership, not philosophical uncertainty.

Through his window, he saw Academy staff and students gathering in the memorial garden. Their faces showed wonder rather than fear as they watched the fountain's impossible patterns. This was what unified magic looked like when people weren't taught to be afraid of it.

His body was weary from the failed experiments, but something deeper troubled him. The Williams family would continue their work, guided by his public theories rather than his private doubts. Future generations would inherit both his discoveries and his carefully maintained silence about what he'd learned too late.

Marcus powered down the last of his experimental systems and secured all records of his personal revelations. The Convergence's energy flowed freely now, seeking its natural patterns without interference. In the garden below, the fountain pulsed with light that spoke of healing rather than destruction.

He settled back in his chair, watching the Academy transform around him. The memorial garden bloomed with new life as unified magic found its natural course. Students laughed as they practiced power that no longer frightened them. Teachers smiled as they discovered possibilities they'd never imagined.

Everything was changing. But the Williams family records would preserve the old certainties, the old fears, the old mission. His descendants would inherit the legacy he'd built in trauma and grief, unchanged by what he'd discovered in his final years.

Perhaps that was for the best. Perhaps some truths were too dangerous to record, too destabilizing to share.

Perhaps the Williams family needed its certainties more than it needed his doubts.

Marcus Williams closed his eyes and let the natural rhythm of restored reality wash over him. His public work was finished, his official choices made. But his private understanding would remain exactly that—private.

The future would inherit both the truth he'd discovered and the lies he'd chosen to preserve.

And only time would tell which would prove stronger.

TWENTY-ONE
WHAT REMAINS

The light faded slowly, existence settling into new patterns around the chamber. Emma's temporal injuries had stabilized completely, and her containment field was no longer necessary as proper time flow restored itself. Where Samantha and Connor had stood, only traces of unified magic remained—golden light and shadow intertwined in the air like a final embrace.

"Commander?" Her voice echoed in the changed space. But she knew there would be no answer. Their sacrifice had been complete, their unified magic given freely to heal what had been broken.

Williams lay curled on the chamber floor. His body was wracked with the aftermath of artificial unification. But his eyes were clear as he watched existence reshape itself around them.

"What have they done?" he whispered. As the cosmos stabilized around them, his scientific mind couldn't deny the evidence before his eyes—unified magic freely given had healed rather than destroyed.

"They saved everything," Emma checked readings on her tablet, watching as existence continued to heal, "by giving themselves to restore what you broke."

Williams stared at his hands, at the burns left by attempting to channel power that was never meant to be artificially unified. "It should have been impossible," he said quietly, his voice hollow, realizing that his life's work might have been built on flawed assumptions. "The calculations... the models... none of them accounted for willing sacrifice. Power freely given rather than forcibly controlled."

His eyes narrowed with renewed determination. "But the risk remains. This unity, this... freedom. Someone must monitor it. Someone must be ready when the inevitable misuse comes." He met Emma's gaze with unexpected intensity. "My work isn't finished. Perhaps it never will be."

The Academy was changing around them. As artificial separation faded, the facility's very structure began to reflect its original purpose—not as a place of control but as a center of learning. The temporal tears had sealed themselves, and proper time flow was restored through willing sacrifice rather than forced separation.

Beyond the chamber windows, they could see the effects spreading. The sky had cleared of reality distortions, and the Convergence's healing energy was now flowing naturally rather than fighting against artificial constraints. Everything that had been broken was becoming whole again.

"The readings are stabilizing," Emma reported, more to herself than to Williams. "Natural harmony returning to existence. The artificial separation is... healing."

"You don't understand what this means." Williams tried to stand but couldn't. The damage from channeling artificial power had left him barely able to move. "Without separation, without control..."

"The cosmos works the way it was meant to work," Emma's voice was firm, "the way it wanted to work before you broke it apart."

Through the chamber's restored windows, they could see other changes beginning. Throughout the Academy and the sector, people remembered. The artificial barriers that had kept unified souls separate were fading, letting natural connections restore themselves.

But not all connections could be restored.

Emma felt tears on her face as she thought of Samantha and Connor. They had given everything they were to heal existence itself. Their unified magic, their merged consciousness, their very beings had become part of the restoration.

"It should have been impossible," Williams said quietly. "The calculations... the power required to restore unity..."

"Was freely given." Emma turned to him. "That's what you never understood. Unity can't be forced or controlled. It has to be chosen, given."

Her tablet chimed with incoming reports. Throughout Federation space, existence stabilized as artificial separation faded. Magic became whole again, working the way it was meant to. The Convergence's healing energy now flowed naturally, restoring rather than fighting.

But the cost...

"Security teams are approaching," she reported, hearing footsteps in the corridor. "What's left of Federation command is trying to understand what's happened."

Williams didn't respond. He was staring at his hands, at the burns left by attempting to channel power that was never meant to be artificially unified.

The security teams that entered were different from the ones that had pursued them earlier. These moved naturally, their magic whole rather than artificially forced together. They took in the changed chamber, the restored existence, the aftermath of sacrifice.

"Commander Carter." The team leader saluted Emma. "We're getting reports from across the sector. Reality patterns are changing; memories are being restored... What happened here?"

Emma looked at the space where Samantha and Connor had stood, where traces of their unified magic still danced in the air.

"They chose to heal rather than break," she said quietly. "Gave themselves completely to restore what was meant to be whole."

"The Federation..." Williams spoke from the floor, his voice weak, "everything we built..."

"Will have to change." Emma watched as the security teams moved to take him into custody. "Build something new, something based on natural unity rather than artificial separation."

Emma felt the weight of command settling onto her shoulders, but differently now. The Academy needed more than just a new leader—it needed someone who understood both what was lost and what could be. Already, ideas were forming about how to restructure magical education around unity rather than division. The old system had to be dismantled carefully and thoughtfully to build something better in its place.

The restoration was still spreading, existence healing itself as artificial constraints faded. Throughout the sector, throughout the galaxy, people were remembering what had been lost, finding connections that had been artificially broken.

But some losses couldn't be restored.

Emma touched the traces of unified magic that still lingered in the air. Golden light and shadow swirled around her fingers, a final echo of what Samantha and Connor had been, what they had chosen to give up to heal everything else.

"Ma'am?" One of the security officers approached carefully. "Command is requesting a full report. They need to understand what's happened—what's still happening as existence... changes."

Reports were coming in from across the sectors—new manifestations of unified magic that didn't fit any known patterns. The restoration hadn't just healed what was broken; it had opened doors to possibilities that even the records hadn't hinted at. And with those possibilities came new dangers and responsibilities. Emma glanced at the data scrolling across her tablet, knowing that somewhere in these reports lay the seeds of their next crisis.

Emma nodded. They would need to know everything—the truth about the Sundering, Williams' attempts to make the separation permanent, and the sacrifice that had healed existence itself.

But most importantly, they needed to understand the price that had been paid, the choice that had been made to restore what was broken.

She took a final look at the chamber where everything had changed, where two people had given everything they were to heal existence itself. To restore natural unity through willing sacrifice rather than forced separation.

Their loss hurt. It would always hurt.

But as she watched existence continue to heal around them and saw natural connections restoring themselves throughout the Academy, throughout the sector, she understood:

Their sacrifice had made everything whole again.

And that was worth any price.

Even the price of letting go.

The future would be different now. It would be whole in a way it hadn't been for centuries, built on willing unity rather than forced separation.

Built on their sacrifice.

Their gift.

Their love.

It would have to be enough.

TWENTY-TWO

NEW DAWN

One month after the restoration, Emma stood in the Academy's central courtyard, watching students practice unified magic. The facility had been transformed, and its very architecture reflected its new purpose as a center for understanding natural unity rather than enforcing artificial separation.

Where the Sundering device had once stood, a memorial garden bloomed. At its heart, a fountain played with streams of water that caught the light like gold and shadow dancing together, a reminder of what had been given to make everything whole again.

Emma watched the fountain's ever-changing patterns with growing fascination. Unlike normal water features, this one never repeated its movements exactly. Sometimes the streams formed complex mathematical equations—the same ones Samantha and Connor had discovered in their Academy research. Other times, the water moved like living magic, golden light and shadow weaving together in ways that seemed almost conscious.

Most intriguing were the moments when the patterns aligned with unified magic formulas. In those instances, the fountain's spray didn't just reflect light—it seemed to generate it from within, creating harmonies that resonated with the restored existence around them. Emma had started keeping detailed records of these occurrences, noting how they intensified during certain astronomical alignments.

"The latest reports are in." Rachel Thompson, her new second-in-command, approached with a data tablet. "Reality patterns have fully stabilized across ninety-seven percent of Federation space. The remaining anomalies are resolving naturally as unified magic restores proper flow."

Emma nodded, watching a young student guide streams of unified magic through complex patterns. No more artificial separation, no more forced division. Just magic working the way it was meant to work.

"And Williams?"

"Still in custody. The tribunal starts next week." Rachel's expression hardened slightly. "He'll have to answer for what he did—what they all did when they broke reality apart."

The Federation itself was changing, restructuring around principles of natural unity rather than artificial control. The truth about the Sundering had shaken centuries of established power, but something better was emerging from the ruins.

"Commander Carter?" a young voice interrupted her thoughts. One of the new students—Jason, she remembered—stood nearby, his unified magic flickering uncertainly around him. "Is it true? About them? About what they did to heal everything?"

Emma felt the familiar ache in her chest but nodded. The students needed to understand what had been sacrificed to give them this chance.

"Their names were Samantha Reed and Connor Blake," she said quietly. "They gave everything they were to heal what had been broken, to restore natural unity through willing sacrifice rather than forced separation."

Jason looked at his hands, at the unified magic dancing around them. "But they're really gone? Even with everything being restored..."

"Some things can't be restored." Emma touched the fountain's water, feeling echoes of unified magic in its flow. "Their sacrifice became part of existence itself, part of what makes everything whole again."

She saw understanding in his young face. These students would grow up in a reality of natural unity, never knowing the artificial constraints that had bound their predecessors. But they needed to understand the price that had been paid for their freedom.

"The memorial service is tomorrow," Rachel reminded her softly. "The whole Academy will attend."

Emma nodded. One month since the restoration. One month since she'd watched her friends give everything they were to heal existence itself. The pain was still fresh, but purpose helped. Understanding helped.

She had work to do.

The Academy's archives had been completely reorganized, now focused on understanding natural unity rather than enforcing separation. The truth about the Sundering was there for anyone to study, along with records of the sacrifice that had healed existence itself.

"Commander?" Another student approached—Lisa, one of their most promising. "We found something in the old records, about unified souls and natural connections..."

Lisa spread out her research materials, her hands trembling with excitement. "Look at these accounts—the Meridian Convergence of 2156, where separated magical pairs across three systems simultaneously achieved reunification, or the Haven Restoration, when unified beings emerged from what everyone thought was destruction." She pointed to specific passages and mathematical proofs that Emma recognized from Samantha and Connor's old work.

"But here's what's fascinating," Lisa continued, pulling up another document. "These aren't just historical accounts. They're patterns, recurring throughout history. The Sundering didn't destroy unified beings—it transformed them. And under the right conditions..." She let the implication hang in the air. "Commander, some of these cases describe pairs returning decades or even centuries later when reality needed them most."

Emma followed her to the archive reading room. Like everything else, the space had been transformed, and it was now bright and open rather than hidden in shadow. On a display screen, texts scrolled past.

"Look," Lisa pointed to specific passages. "When they broke everything apart, split magic and souls... some connections were too strong to completely separate. Some unified souls found each other despite everything they did to keep them apart."

"Like Commanders Reed and Blake," Rachel added quietly.

"Yes." Emma studied the texts. "But there's more. The records suggest... suggest that truly unified souls can't be permanently separated. That even complete sacrifice might not be..."

Emma studied the passage more closely. There were references to other unified souls throughout history who had seemingly vanished during great magical workings, only to re-emerge when they were most needed.

The technical details were compelling. The Rahman-Santos pair, thought destroyed in the Outer Rim crisis, manifested a century later to prevent a catastrophic cosmic collapse. The Morgan-Wei Collective hadn't been eliminated by Federation forces—they'd transformed themselves to heal a sector-wide magical corruption. Each case followed similar patterns: apparent sacrifice led not to destruction but to transformation, unified beings choosing to become part of existence itself until conditions allowed their return.

Emma's tactical training recognized the implications. The fountain's increasingly complex patterns, the way certain magical harmonics were strengthening rather than fading, and the mathematical resonance seemed to pulse stronger with each passing day. These weren't just echoes of what had been lost—they were signs of something building.

The records were fragmented but clear on one point: true unity, freely given, was never truly lost—only transformed.

"There's more," Lisa said, her voice dropping to a whisper. "The patterns in the fountain—I've been mapping them against these historical accounts." She pulled up a complex chart showing energy fluctuations over time. "Commander, the mathematical signatures are identical. Whatever happened to those other unified pairs, the same resonance patterns are appearing here."

Emma stared at the data, her pulse quickening. "You're saying..."

"I'm saying the fountain isn't just a memorial." Lisa's eyes were bright with discovery. "It's a focal point. The same kind of energy nexus that preceded every recorded return. And it's getting stronger."

The implications hit Emma like a physical blow. She looked out the window toward the memorial garden, where water danced in patterns that never repeated, where light and shadow played together in ways that seemed almost alive.

"Keep monitoring it," she said quietly. "Record everything. And Lisa? Keep this between us for now. Until we understand what it means."

The young woman nodded, already turning back to her research with renewed intensity. Emma left the archives, her mind spinning with possibilities she didn't dare voice aloud.

Outside, she found herself drawn back to the fountain. Students had gathered around it, some practicing their unified magic, others simply watching the endless dance of water and light. The patterns seemed more complex today, more purposeful.

A new thought struck her. She pulled out her tablet and began cross-referencing the fountain's activity with Federation reports from across the galaxy. As the data populated, a clear pattern emerged: every spike in the fountain's energy corresponded with a new manifestation of unified magic somewhere in Federation space. Not random occurrences, but a spreading wave of awakening, as if the fountain were somehow catalyzing the return of natural unity across the galaxy.

"Commander?" Rachel approached with another report. "We're getting some interesting readings from the outer territories. New academies requesting guidance on handling unified magic students. It seems the restoration is having effects far beyond what we initially calculated."

Emma smiled, watching a particularly complex pattern form in the fountain's spray. "Good. The universe is remembering how to be whole. Our job is to help it remember safely."

But even as she spoke, part of her mind was elsewhere, processing Lisa's research and the mounting evidence that something unprecedented was building. The fountain pulsed with energy that grew stronger each day. The historical records suggested a pattern of return that defied death itself. And somewhere in the dance of light and shadow, she thought she could almost sense...

"Ma'am?" A security officer approached. "The memorial preparations are complete. The service tomorrow will be broadcast sector-wide."

Emma nodded, but her attention remained on the fountain. Tomorrow they would honor the sacrifice that had saved everything. But if Lisa's research was correct, if the patterns held true, then perhaps that sacrifice wasn't as final as they'd believed.

As evening approached, Emma made her final rounds through the Academy. In every corridor, she saw evidence of the new reality Samantha and Connor had died to create. Students of all backgrounds working together, their magic flowing naturally without artificial constraints. Teachers developing new curricula based on unity rather than separation. Even the building itself seemed different, its architecture somehow more harmonious, more whole.

She paused at the central tower, where Williams had once conducted his experiments. The space had been converted into a research center focused on understanding natural magical harmony. Plaques on the wall honored all those who had died fighting for truth, with Samantha and Connor's names prominently displayed.

But it was the smaller inscription below that caught her attention: "In memory of those who gave freely, and in hope of reunion when the cosmos calls them home."

The words had been suggested by one of the students, based on passages from the historical accounts Lisa had discovered. At the time, Emma had thought them poetic but meaningless. Now, she wondered if they might be prophetic.

The fountain's song seemed to grow louder as night fell, its patterns more luminous in the darkness. Emma stood before it one last time before heading to her quarters, watching water and light dance together in configurations that spoke of mathematics beyond human understanding.

"Wherever you are," she whispered to the dancing patterns, "know that your sacrifice wasn't in vain. The reality you died to save is growing into something beautiful."

The fountain pulsed once, brighter than usual, and for just a moment Emma could have sworn she heard familiar voices in the water's song—not words, but emotions. Love. Hope. The promise that some bonds transcend even death itself.

She touched the water one last time, feeling the resonance that grew stronger each day. Tomorrow would bring the memorial service, and with it the formal end of one chapter in the Academy's history. But as she walked away, Emma carried with her the growing certainty that another chapter was already beginning to write itself.

In the dance of light and shadow, in the fountain's never-ending patterns, in the spreading wave of unified magic across the galaxy, something was building. Something that honored the past while reaching toward an impossible future.

The fountain played on through the night, its song of hope echoing through the Academy halls. And somewhere in the spaces between moments, in the flow of restored unity, two souls continued their eternal dance.

Together.

Always.

Even in the dawn of what was yet to come.

NOTE FROM THE AUTHOR

Thank you so much for reading. If you enjoyed this book I'd really love it if you could leave a 30 second review on Amazon.

Here is a QR code to the review page.

ABOUT THE AUTHOR

Richard French represents a rare convergence of high-tech leadership, competitive motorsports, and literary achievement. With over 20 years of global C-suite experience, Richard has been recognized as one of the country's foremost authorities on Robotic Process Automation and AI Automation. His executive journey includes senior leadership roles at Oracle and Nokia, CEO positions at multiple successful startups, and the distinction of guiding companies from early-stage ventures to organizations earning over $100 million annually. His expertise spans five continents, where he's built and led teams across diverse markets and cultures.

Beyond the boardroom, Richard channels his passion for precision and performance into GT race car driving, competing across the United States in the Porsche Sprint Challenge Series West. This unique combination of analytical thinking from technology and high-stakes decision-making from racing profoundly influences his approach to writing and leadership philosophy.

Richard's literary portfolio demonstrates remarkable versatility, encompassing his flagship business leadership book "*Daniel as a Blueprint for Navigating Ethical Dilemmas,*" other business ethics guides like "*Proverbs for Profit,*" comprehensive journaling resources including "The Journaling Mastery Series", and "*The Journaling Prompts Series*", biblical studies such as "*Revelation Explained: Verse by Verse,*" and his expansion into speculative fiction with *The Convergence Series*, featuring "*Broken Magic*" and

"*Restoration*." His mathematics degree from a top Canadian university and decades of explaining complex technological innovations have honed his ability to make intricate concepts accessible to diverse audiences. Now retired and enjoying the freedom to focus on his passion for writing, Richard lives in the Pacific Northwest with his wife and two Boston Terriers, Reggie and Tilly.

facebook.com/richardfrenchauthor
instagram.com/richardfrenchauthor
tiktok.com/@richardfrenchauthor
youtube.com/@richardfrenchwrites